Poison Rage

The Rage Trilogy: Book 2

by

William Blackwell

Cover Designed by Telemachus Press, LLC

Published by Telemachus Press, LLC

ISBN: 978-1-0697318-1-4 (paperback)

Version: 2017.01.01

Acknowledgements

Heartfelt thanks to my loyal and supportive readers, friends and family, the hardworking staff at Telemachus Press, and Winslow Eliot. Special thanks to the Government of Prince Edward Island for its financial support.

To my loyal supporters, without whose help I could not continue to create.

Poison Rage

The Rage Trilogy: Book 2

Another Day

One eye open, one eye closed.
  Choose to rise, choose to doze.
  Slowly moving, quick to think.
  It's your time to swim or sink.
  Go on in, they're there you'll see.
  Hold your breath, count to three.
  Closest table, closest chair.
  Don't look around, try not to stare.
  Take it in, the sights, the sounds.
  Are my feet still touching the ground?
  Get a grip, hold on tight.
  What am I feeling?
  Is it right?
  Thoughts are spinning, hands are shaking.
  Will they know that I am faking?
  All I really want to be, is someone with
  some certainty.
  Give it up, let it be.
  Take a chance, just be me.
  Eyes are closed, it's alright.
  Another day, another fright.
  One day down, more to go.
  Lights are off, that ends the show.
  –Anonymous

Chapter One

Kathleen Freeborne opened her eyes slowly to bright lights shining intrusively on her. *Where am I? How long have I been here? What happened?* She strained her aching mind to try and make sense of events, but nothing came to her, only disconnected images, some violent and surreal. She knew one thing—her head throbbed from a hangover.

I'm in you and you're in me.

She felt her heart rate quicken, took deep breaths to try and slow it down, something her counselor Betty Shifert—a recent addition to her life—had told her would help. She blinked and studied her unfamiliar surroundings, a private hospital room. *Where?* She picked up a food menu sitting on a serving table next to her bed, flipped it over and read: *King's County Memorial Hospital, Montague, PEI.*

Shit, I'm in the hospital. How did I get here? Then she remembered. She and boyfriend Mark Riley, along with paranormal team members and friends Angela Dodson and Jacob McCreery, had gone to Poverty Beach last night, July 1, 2012, to celebrate Canada Day, the date in 1867 that Canada was officially united into a single country.

The evening had begun innocently enough, the four sitting on a small blanket around a campfire, laughing, drinking, enjoying the evening stars and listening to the portable stereo belt out rock 'n roll tunes from *Ocean 100* radio station. But then something had gone terribly wrong. A strange old woman had appeared out of nowhere, offering them a drink of some potent moonshine she was drunkenly swilling.

Angela, Jacob, and Kathleen had no interest in the potion, but Mark had decided to indulge. After a few swigs he had ripped off his t-shirt and started a ritualistic chant while dancing around the fire, his eyes wild and far away. The old woman, who had not offered her name as far as Kathleen could remember, had disappeared by that time. And her memory of the woman's appearance had been vague at best. It had been dark. She had been drunk.

Mark's chants became more violent as he danced, at one point extracting a fiery torch and waving it dangerously close to his friends' faces.

Finally his chants, some incomprehensible gibberish, had transformed into shrieks of rage and his eyes had widened, turning a fiery red. That's when he had started poking Jacob with the flaming torch, taunting and threatening him.

"Burn in hell, you son of a bitch," he had said, poking the torch closer, closer to Jacob, at one point lighting the cuff of his pants on fire.

That's when Kathleen had lost it and began yelling at her boyfriend to snap out of it. She remembered Angela had also gotten quite upset and had called someone, probably Detective Blaine Redmond, who involuntary had become a knight in shining armor in many of Prince Edward Island Paranormal Investigators (PEIPI) cases.

But, other than becoming angry and upset at her boyfriend attacking Jacob with the flame, Kathleen could remember little else. *I must have had a panic attack and passed out. That's why I'm here. Mark and the others. Where are they?*

Her physician Frank Heeling walked into the room holding a chart and greeted her with a smile. "How are you?"

"My head hurts. But otherwise okay. Mark, the others, do you know what happened?"

"I just had a conversation with Detective Redmond in the hallway," the doctor said, absently running a hand through his wild Albert Einstein-style mop of hair. "He may want to talk to you later, if you're up to it?"

Silence. Finally Kathleen nodded. Her heart rate quickened. *What happened? Something went wrong. Did Mark kill Jacob?*

Heeling took a seat bedside and put a hand on her arm. "Deep breaths. I'm sure everything's going to be okay."

"Tell me what happened, please," she said, eying the doctor anxiously.

"Angela and Jacob are fine. But right now Mark Riley is missing."

Kathleen felt the pain in her lower back first and winced as it slowly trickled up her spine. *Not another one. Fight it.*

Heeling produced a Thorazine pill, placed it gently in her hand and offered her a glass of water. "Here. Take this."

She swallowed the pill quickly, closed her eyes and fought to control the panic attack rising up, threatening to send her into a catatonic and useless state. "*Hang in there, dear. You'll be okay,*" a voice inside her head said. She recognized Elizabeth Pelletier's voice and shivered. *Will this woman ever leave me?*

"*Not until it's all over,*" came the response. "*For now, I'm in you and you're in me.*"

"Are you okay?" Heeling asked, concern etched in his furrowed brow. Kathleen's eyes had become distant, unfocused.

"I'm fine," she said, struggling to regain control of her senses. She had no idea if she would ever be fine again in her life.

Chapter Two

What kind of a messed up life is this? Mark thought, tugging at the rope that bound his arms the next afternoon. It only cinched tighter and he winced in pain. He had just opened his eyes and slowly become aware of his surroundings. He was in a dark cellar, his arms outstretched and tied to iron hooks that had been drilled into the concrete wall. His legs were bound tightly together with rope. He blinked, adjusting to the darkness in the room. But for a ray of sunlight penetrating a crack in an old wooden exit door at the top of some rickety stairs, the cellar was black. It smelled damp and musty. The only sounds he heard were the faint chirping of birds outside, merrily discussing the merits of summer.

He could also hear the faint barking of a dog, a large dog judging by the bark.

How the fuck did I get here? But for a pair of torn denim shorts he was naked. He tried to recollect the events that might have brought him here. He remembered partying with his friends at Poverty Beach but not much else. They were celebrating Canada Day and the purchase of a new house he had just bought with Kathleen with an insurance settlement, the result of a rear-end collision that continued to give him back pain.

They were also celebrating the union of Angela and Jacob, who had also bought a house together, after Angela had finally sold the haunted house she inherited from her deceased grandfather. After one too many threats, and in two cases actual physical violence from a psychotic apparition intent on having his way with her, she decided it was in the best interest of her mental health to sell the property. Her realtor had even noted in the public comments on the Multiple Listing Service, the home "comes complete with Casper the friendly ghost."

A ghost inhabited the property all right. But he was pretty far from friendly.

We were drinking and having a great time but then what? Slowly his mind started to fill in an important gap. An old woman had appeared and offered them some moonshine. Did the others drink it? He couldn't remember. But he did remember sampling it, indulging in more than one large swig.

But he couldn't remember a single thing after that. Was it the alcohol? He couldn't be sure, but he suspected there was more to it than that. And the old woman. Hadn't he seen her before, walking down Main Street Montague, pushing a shopping cart, a collection of clothing, other odds and ends, inside it? He thought she looked familiar. What was her name?

The door suddenly creaked open and Beatrice Maling slowly hobbled down the rickety stairs, a black cane thumping alongside her. The cellar was illuminated briefly as a large yellow sunbeam shone inside the dark hole, but was enveloped in blackness again as the door slammed shut behind her. She fidgeted with the only source of light, a dangling light fixture, finally turning the bulb on.

Momentarily blinded as his eyes adjusted to the incandescent light, Mark blinked, trying to see the hunched-over figure hobbling toward him. Her wrinkled face, crooked grin, thin grey long hair, slowly came into focus.

"What do you want with me?" Mark said as she approached.

"You and your group made a big mistake," she said, waving the cane dangerously close to his head.

"What are you talking about?"

"You put an end to my great-grandfather, Reverend James Maling," she said, smacking him hard in the nose with the rubberized butt-end of the cane, like an angry old teacher cross with a student caught cheating on an exam.

Mark screamed in pain, felt the warm blood from the cut on his nose drip down his face, onto his chin, neck, and chest. *I think she broke my nose.*

The memory of James Maling was too fresh in his mind to forget it anytime soon; even with the passage of many years he would never be able to forget how that evil, devil-worshiping apparition had possessed and cold-bloodedly murdered almost a hundred residents of this otherwise peaceful island province. A macabre and grisly scene worthy of a million horrific nightmares.

If it wasn't for PEIPI and Detective Blaine Redmond, who knew how long the murderous rampage would have continued? Of course it was the apparition of Elizabeth Pelletier, who had been brutally raped and murdered by James Maling in the late 1800's, who had possessed Kathleen, led Detective Redmond to the whereabouts of the demented psycho apparition and, with the power of the ancient sword, finally released him back into the spirit world—condemned him to hell with any luck.

Was he back? Mark didn't know. But he knew one thing. One of Maling's descendants was here and hell-bent on revenge. Mark shuddered at the thought, fought hard to control the panic rising up inside his chest. *Isn't it my girlfriend who suffers from panic attacks? Where is she? Does this psycho have her? Better play along.* "Don't hurt me. I'll help you. What do you want me to do?"

"You don't have a choice in the matter, young man," she said, cackling long and hard. She turned, hobbled to a small wooden table that Mark noticed for the very first time. It was full of small vials, larger bottles of liquid, a number of small dolls, the accoutrements of black magic, modern-day witchcraft.

She returned with a small doll, sewn of cloth and vaguely resembling Mark. *Me. No, that's not me. That's a fucking doll. This can't be happening.*

She produced a pin from the pocket of her black granny dress, held it up and paused, waiting for some acknowledgement from her prisoner.

The thin metal glinted in the incandescent light, the light fixture still swaying slowly from its cord.

"No," Mark said, feeling an adrenaline rush of fear. "You don't have to do that. I'll help you."

She pierced the small pin into the right arm of the doll and Mark winced and screamed in pain, noticing a small puncture wound in his right bicep that was now beginning to drip blood on the dirt floor.

She extracted the pin, smiling wickedly. "Are we on the same page now?"

Mark felt another bolt of pain, his eyes narrowing. "Yes we are. What do you want from me?"

"I want you to lead your friends to another paranormal investigation," she said. "The whole team."

He paused momentarily and she pointed the pin at the doll's head.

"Okay, okay," he said quickly and fearfully. "Where and when?"

"The woman's name is Eva Santire and she'll be calling you in a few days. She'll give you the address and explain everything."

"Okay, I'll do it. Who are you anyway?"

"None of that is important right now. You'll find out soon enough, once you've been indoctrinated."

She pointed to the wooden table on which four or five other dolls were placed. She threw the injured doll hastily on the table and Mark felt a bolt of pain shoot up his lower back.

"Careful with that," he said after the pain had subsided a little.

She picked up another doll. "Do you know who this is?"

"I think I can guess."

"Go ahead."

"Kathleen."

"Right, and if you deviate from the plan in any way, or open your mouth and tell people, she gets this pin here right through her heart." She waived the pin threateningly. "And your other friends will meet the same fate. And don't think for a minute you won't be watched."

Beatrice turned to the table, lit a small candle, brought out an empty vial, emptied powdery and liquid contents from the other vials into it and started uttering phrases, incomprehensible to Mark, but evidently they had some connection to the potion she was mixing up. Her eyes glowed eerily as she neared the end of her chant, holding the concoction in front of her face, saying, "This spell will last until the magic word is spoken, and then and only then will it be broken."

She picked up the Kathleen Voodoo doll by the throat, held the potion in the other hand and approached Mark. "Drink this now without a fuss and I promise I won't throttle your little missy."

Mark's jaw dropped and eyes widened as she approached, the crop of goose bumps starting at his ankles and sprouting quickly over his entire body.

He nodded slowly and swallowed the potion, wondering if his life would ever be the same.

Chapter Three

Will my life ever be the same? Police Detective Blaine Redmond wondered grimly the next afternoon, listening to the litany of complaints from his troubled wife, Jeanette. Since the murderous events of a few months ago, he doubted it. Some of the people who died in the carnage had been his good friends. Bill Blythe, for example, a happy-go-lucky caretaker, had joined in many of his coffee and donut yak sessions with other policemen at Tim Horton's in Montague, a few short blocks from where he lived.

He was haunted by memories of Bill, the cheerful old soul, who had become possessed by the evil spirit of reverend James Maling and turned into a sadistic and ruthless killer. Haunted by the last image he had of the man whose life he had ended with a few well-aimed bullets from his handgun, bullets that had penetrated deep into Bill's heart and took his life a few short years after semi-retirement. What haunted him most was the transformation that had taken place in the man as he drew his last breath. Just before dying he had transformed into the Bill Blythe of old, the friendly soul that Redmond had enjoyed so many interesting conversations with.

And that was only the beginning.

There were a few other friends who had been unlucky recipients of fatal gunshots fired by the detective. All had been possessed, all had been necessary.

Or so he told himself to justify it.

And then there was the fatal inferno at the old church that had put an untimely end to the lives of many of his friends and acquaintances.

There was a time in his career that he wished for that one big case, the one that would make him famous, and fast-track his career to a promotion. Now, with all the carnage and murder he had endured of late, his ambition had all but abandoned him. At thirty-nine-years-old, Redmond felt old before his time, washed up, and cynical.

Once a skeptic of the paranormal, he now regarded everyone he met with suspicion, searching for a clue that would indicate they were possessed. Maybe he dropped the ball during his previous investigation, pointing to himself as the one in some way responsible for all the carnage, or maybe he had lost faith in humanity and become disillusioned with life in general.

He didn't know.

But he knew he had become despondent with his wife of six years, slowly paying less and less attention to her, until finally he had become content with his own company, his own wallowing, his own bottle of beer.

He couldn't blame Jeanette for becoming angry and upset with him. After all, she had lost her best friend, Anne Blanchard, in the blaze, and needed some consoling of her own. Only trouble was, Redmond was in no mental condition to give it to her.

Not now, possibly not ever.

Sitting on a soft comfortable lawn chair in his garden, sipping a beer in the hot afternoon sun, he finally stared at Jeanette, an attractive woman with short brown hair, trying to understand what she was saying. He had tuned her out again, as he often had lately.

"I'm sorry, honey, what were you saying?"

Her face reddened as she shot him an annoyed expression, her cute dimples becoming more pronounced. They always did that when she was angry. "Are you ever going to start listening to me? It would be nice if you would focus on us once in a while. I was saying you've changed in a bad way. Look at this lawn. We have to pay someone to cut it now. You used to love gardening. And the house. If I wasn't working double-time keeping it clean, it would be an absolute pigsty. You used to help me and clean up after yourself. And your job. Since when would you ever drink beer before going to work? Now look at you. How many have you had?"

"This is my second," he lied. He had hidden the first three empties in the garage just before Jeanette had arrived home after finishing her shift as a nurse at the hospital.

She eyed him skeptically. She could always tell when he was lying. But it was a question of pick your battles. She didn't question him on that.

Redmond suddenly remembered Mark Riley was still missing, two days after he had questioned Kathleen on his possible whereabouts. Other than a vague description of the old lady, who didn't resemble anyone the detective thought he knew, Kathleen hadn't provided anything substantial. And then he remembered Poverty Beach, the scene of the disappearance. He hadn't even returned to the scene of the crime to search for clues.

He made some small talk with Jeanette, promised to bring home dinner later and spend the evening together uninterrupted, drained the last mouthful of beer, kissed her perfunctorily on the cheek and left.

Jeanette frowned. One small tear was visible in her right eye as the detective walked away.

Feeling slightly buzzed and a little wrung-out, Redmond vlimbed in his black cruiser and headed toward Poverty Beach. The day was calm and sunny, and a few popcorn clouds dotted the otherwise clear blue sky. He glanced at the calm waters of the Atlantic Ocean as he weaved along the scenic coastal highway heading east from town. Pale blue waters that at one time calmed his nerves now did little to brighten his somber spirits.

A few minutes later he pulled onto the small dirt road that would take him out to the secluded sand spit that was Poverty Beach. He parked his car, closed the door, and suddenly remembered what he had forgotten. He had taken to driving around with a small six-pack cooler in the trunk of his car. When his troubled mind got the better of him, he would pull over in one of the many park areas dotting the coast, knock back a few until he felt numb enough to continue, and then carry on with his day.

He had planned to kill a few hours at the beach with a few cold ones before checking into the station. He was a seasoned detective and was pretty much left on his own to conduct his investigations, only showing up when he wanted or needed to. Unlike some of the other duty cops, Redmond didn't punch the clock.

But the domestic problems at home had permeated his mind prior to leaving and he had left the cooler, full of ice and beer, inside the garage. Forgotten it. *Like a lot of things lately*, he thought, poking around the small campfire PEIPI had celebrated at prior to Mark's disappearance.

He kicked around the charred embers and a bottle rolled out, shaped like nothing he had ever seen before. It was a clear glass bottle, wide at the bottom, swirling up narrower at the top. It had a clear raised image of an airborne bat. It was obviously antique, the glass thick and sturdy in his hands. There was a drop or two of yellow liquid in the bottom and he held it to his nose. He instantly recoiled at the smell and a wave of nausea swept through him. He felt something like rage begin to boil up inside of him and instinctively threw the bottle on the sand and it twirled in a circle for a moment before stopping.

His senses slowly cleared and the hateful emotions passed. He took a deep breath, turned, and walked down the beach. *I'll get it when I return. I don't want to touch it right now.*

He noticed what first appeared to be a man sun-tanning on the beach. Gentle waves lapped his body, falling just short of washing over his head. But, nearing, he realized the man wasn't moving. Coming closer, he recognized the face of Mark Riley. He knelt down to feel for a pulse and noticed Mark's nose was out of joint, clearly broken. Blood had scabbed up around his nostrils, some of it crusted to his lips.

He felt for a pulse. There was one. Mark was alive. "Hey Mark," he said, gently shaking his arm.

In a moment, Mark opened his eyes and stared at the detective, slowly recognizing him.

"Are you okay?" Redmond asked. His ice cold six-pack would have to wait until he filed a report.

Mark blinked, bringing his hand to his nose. *What the fuck just happened?*

"No, don't touch it," Redmond said. "I think it's broken. Let's get you to the hospital."

He helped Mark to the car, loaded him into the passenger seat and closed the door. Mark blankly stared out the window as Redmond retrieved the bottle with a gloved hand, dropped it into a plastic bag, and put it gently in the trunk.

He caught a small whiff of the contents before he sealed the evidence bag and stood outside the vehicle for a few minutes, waiting for the gnawing feelings of hostility and rage to dissipate. *Poison rage!*

"What happened to you?" Redmond said as they pulled away.

"I don't remember."

Chapter Four

"I don't remember," Kathleen told counselor Betty Shifert as they sat in the small office late the following afternoon. Kathleen had been released from the hospital yesterday and had taken today off from work to try and compose herself for the remainder of the week.

Although a slightly drunk Blaine Redmond had delivered her boyfriend to her yesterday after a trip to the hospital to reset his broken nose, she still felt the ever-present edge, now compounded by the knowledge that she was possessed by the spirit of Elizabeth Pelletier, who surely must be hanging around for a reason. This woman had helped rid the town of the evil presence of Reverend James Maling in the past, but why hadn't she left?

Because it's not over, that's why. And Mark has somehow become unwittingly indoctrinated into the next evil plan. Why can't he remember anything?

"You don't remember anything?" Betty asked, looking over her horn-rimmed spectacles, taking copious notes and occasionally glancing out the window at the greenery, the sunlit afternoon, the people going about their business on the street below. She was about fifty-five with thick brown hair arranged in a bun. She had pleasant features and a pleasant disposition. She was a little overweight, but she hid it well with a white lab coat, and the image she presented reminded Kathleen more of a lab technician than a counselor. *Oh well. Each to their own.*

Kathleen shook her head.

Betty was trying to pinpoint, during the night of Mark's disappearance, exactly when her mind had gone blank and how long the gap lasted. "So, after you started yelling at Mark to stop attacking your friends, you drew a blank?"

Kathleen nodded. So far she had managed to keep her friend Elizabeth Pelletier out of the picture and she wanted to keep it that way. Shifert might lock her in a padded room and throw away the key for all she knew.

"And what did you feel just before blanking out?"

"All kinds of nasty thoughts," Kathleen said, twisting her head, wondering why her neck had suddenly stiffened. "Like my life was coming to an end, my relationship was going to fail. I'm going to get fired, bills piling up, things like that."

There was a pause. "But some of these thoughts seem to be premonitions," Betty said, looking over her notes. "You've just been through a rather grueling experience and it seems to me some of that might have been foretold in the voices you heard during your panic attacks."

Kathleen had paid the voices some attention before, and she had to admit some of them had proven to be premonitions.

Shifert switched the line of questioning. "How have you been sleeping?"

"I haven't been sleeping well for the last month."

"Do you think it's the medication?"

"I don't know."

"How do you feel about the medication? Is it working?"

"Sometimes yes and sometimes no. It makes me drowsy so I'd like to get off it, if possible."

"Do you have any history of depression? Or, have you been depressed lately? Are you depressed now?"

"No, no, and no," Kathleen said, starting to wish for an end to this session.

"Considering all the people who died a few months back, you would have every reason to be going through a grieving period, to be depressed."

"I miss some of my friends, but I'm not depressed."

"What about work? Any problems there?"

Kathleen was reluctant to go into a lot of detail about her work situation. She still felt the gossip grapevine could potentially put her in danger if she said too much. She had no idea if Betty had friends at the school where Kathleen worked as an education assistant, helping children with autism overcome their learning disabilities. And teacher Ron Baglund had been using restraints on some of the kids lately, restraints that had not been approved by the union or the school board. Kathleen had made the mistake of emailing her concern to Baglund a few days before being admitted into the hospital and had not heard anything back. She was afraid when she went into work tomorrow that there would be a blow-up with Baglund and he would interpret the email as a personal attack on him, dragging up all the little issues of the past few months that called into question his teaching skills.

In retrospect, Kathleen thought it would have been better to confront Baglund, but part of her was afraid of him. After all, hadn't the control freak yelled and screamed at the education assistants in the past, right in front of the students, during a classroom session? Yes, he had.

But in the end, she had reasoned that it would be easy for tone to get misinterpreted in text and email. In this case, a conversation would have been much better. She had not handled the situation well and was sure tomorrow would bring a violent explosion that would serve to confirm her gut instinct.

"Nothing that I can't handle," Kathleen said, hoping she sounded convincing.

"Okay," Betty said, closing the file on her desk. "Ultimately Doctor Heeling will make the call on your medication. But if you'd like to get off them, I'll try and help you." She wrote something on a piece of paper and handed it to Kathleen.

"It's called Adrenasmart," Betty said. "It's an herbal supplement that calms the nervous system and helps you sleep. I take it myself sometimes. You can buy it without a prescription."

Kathleen pocketed the paper, thanked the counselor, made a mental note about her appointment next week and walked out the door into the bright sunlight.

Such a beautiful day but everything was wrong. She was possessed by a benevolent spirit, Mark was acting strangely, something bad was about to happen, she just knew it, and Ron Baglund would certainly confront her tomorrow and blow up in her face. She might even lose her job. She couldn't remember ever having a year in her life this stressful and sometimes she thought of leaving everything behind, leaving the small town of Montague and starting over somewhere else.

Is that what she needed? A change? She didn't know anymore.

Chapter Five

"I didn't know you weren't in the mood," Jacob said as he stared at Angela's back. It was early evening and they were lying in bed together in their new two-story home in Montague. The evening had started off romantic enough; a candlelit dinner, a bottle of red wine, and scented candles around the king-sized bed. Dinner had gone well, light conversation, laughter, and while Jacob was putting away the dishes Angela had come up behind him, enveloping him in a tight hug, teasingly kissing his neck and ear—something she knew drove him crazy.

He had turned around, kissed her passionately, and they had raced up to the candlelit bedroom, diving into the comfortable new bed. But after some heavy petting, Angela had abruptly stopped, stared at him blankly for a few seconds and turned away.

And it wasn't the first time it had happened. When they had first taken possession of their new home a few months ago, their relationship had been idyllic: Excellent sex, a great friendship, mutual attraction, trust and respect—the foundation of a great relationship.

But slowly over the last month a few cracks had appeared in that foundation—the mortar had started to crumble. Jacob at first had not realized how psychologically scarred Angela was from the abusive relationship she had suffered at the hands of her ex-husband, Aaron.

It added insult to injury that she had been sexually assaulted by a demented ghost in the old house her grandfather had left her in his will. Hell, the ghost had even tried to kill her, strangling her to within a few seconds of losing her life.

What made it worse was they had not been able to determine the ghost's identity. Their historical analysis had netted zero results. Sometimes, learning the identity of the person behind the attacks helps a victim deal with it. In some cases, the abusive spirit can even be released back into the spirit world, or sent straight to hell in a handbasket, preventing the spirit from ever being able to harm anyone else. But in this case that hadn't happened, and Jacob suspected it gnawed at Angela, knowing that the young couple who had bought the house might be in some kind of danger.

He also worried that the scars she bore from the physical and sexual abuse might never heal. Angela could be hot one minute, cold the next, changing on a dime. A few weeks ago, during one such cold-chill infusion, Jacob had suggested Angela see a counselor. But she wouldn't hear of it, insisting she would heal in her own time. *How long is her own time?*

Jacob didn't know. But he did know that he was starting to become impatient. While sex wasn't everything, it was certainly, at least for him, an integral component of a healthy relationship. He enjoyed getting lost in carnal pleasure with the woman he loved. But, for the last month, the carnal pleasure had become less and less frequent. According to Jacob's calculations, they hadn't made love in almost a month. Sure, they had come close a few times. But the ending had been the same. Angela had turned off abruptly like a faucet, instantly cutting off the flow of passion, not even a drop of desire visible.

Along with sexual frustration, the other thing bothering Jacob was the slow but steady progress of the black cloud of depression he had suffered after breaking off with his last girlfriend over infidelity issues. When he had initially consummated his relationship with Angela, fallen madly in love really, the black cloud had all but disappeared and his first month had been one of conjugal bliss.

But now, he noticed it again lurking in the back of his head, waiting for his attention, so it could envelop his mind, sap his energy, strip away his motivation, render him listless, lifeless and sad. It had yet to fully announce itself in debilitating fashion, but it was there alright and lately every day was a fight to keep it at bay.

He didn't want to think about it now. So he got up, walked into the bathroom and splashed some cold water on his face.

"What're you doing?" Angela said from the bedroom, rolling over, her white undershirt exposing ample cleavage of a fine set of breasts.

"I'm going to do some work," he said, leaving the bedroom and going into his office.

At his desk, he thought of calling Mark, whom he knew had just been released from hospital after mysteriously reappearing a few days after his equally mysterious disappearance. He also thought of calling Kathleen, whose panic attacks had become much more debilitating and violent than in the past. They had been through a lot. And they were all handling it in their own ways, for better or worse. *I'll call them tomorrow.*

He knew work always helped to control the black cloud so he decided to throw himself into a new website he was designing for a client. But a few minutes later, his mind became distracted and he started thinking about Angela's deceased grandfather, Jim Dodson. Who else might have occupied the house who would have a reason to inflict such terror into the hearts and minds of his victims? Wait a minute. Didn't Jim have a brother who had stayed with him? Wasn't his name Raymond? Jacob was sure Angela had mentioned Raymond previously, describing him as a black sheep of the family whom she knew little about. This called for some more research. Was it possible Raymond had a dark past that was being concealed from Angela's family?

Jacob didn't know. But he was certainly going to find out. It was worth a shot. As he was punching the name into Google, he noticed his phone vibrating across his desk. It was Kathleen. He looked at the clock: 9:26 pm. *What could she possibly want at this hour?* He picked it up.

"Jacob, you up for a paranormal investigation tonight?" Kathleen said.

These people must be crazy. They both just got released from hospital. "Sure," he said without hesitation.

Chapter Six

There was some hesitation in Kathleen's voice as she provided details to Mark, Jacob and Angela. They sat in the trustworthy truck Black Death outside an 1896 bungalow, about an hour later on a small wooded lot on the outskirts of town.

The sky was black. The stars glittered, the moon full and beaming in the still night.

A woman, Anne Poletsky, had called Kathleen earlier in the evening in a panic, explaining she had witnessed her elderly mother Maria being shaken violently in a rocking chair by a small girl, who had later disappeared into the basement of the house. Anne, who lived with her husband and two kids about a mile from Maria, had been over visiting when the attack happened. She also claimed Maria had seen apparitions of her deceased husband Bruce, who would make the odd appearance usually accompanied by some kind of practical joke. Just last night, according to Anne, her mother had seen the apparition of Bruce in her bedroom and he had stripped the bed of its blankets while Maria was trying to sleep.

Anne also claimed to have seen apparitions of the little girl on other occasions, including one night while she was sleeping over at her mother's house, the girl had appeared at her bedside, waking her up by playing a flute.

Anne didn't know who the little girl was, but desperately wanted the team to contact her. And she earnestly wanted PEIPI to contact her father Bruce as well.

Initially Kathleen wanted to schedule the investigation for another night. She had had enough drama lately. But, listening to the panic in Anne's voice, she had acquiesced. Since the team helped locate and destroy the evil presence of James Maling they had become celebrities in the small town. Kathleen knew many locals viewed her as something of a clairvoyant, and a damned good one at that.

They nodded as she finished her explanation, exited the truck, and began loading gear into the house.

The team set up video cameras and audio recorders while Kathleen sat in the living room with Anne and Maria discussing some of the strange happenings.

"You know most people would think I'm crazy if I told them this stuff," Anne said. "My husband doesn't believe in ghosts and he just laughs when I tell him about the little girl." Anne was in her fifties, pleasantly plump, with long black hair and inquisitive brown eyes. Her mother Maria sat silently while she talked, occasionally glancing at Kathleen. Just shy of 90, Maria had mid-length grey hair, a wrinkled face and pleasing disposition. She looked like an honest woman, a good person. Kathleen's impression of the daughter was the same.

Anne had also explained her mother was recovering from a recent stroke, which made Kathleen wonder about the validity of the elderly woman's information.

"How was your relationship with your husband?" Kathleen asked.

"It was good," Maria said, her eyes glancing around the room as if waiting for his ghost to return.

"When and how did he die?"

"Four years ago," Maria said. "He had a heart attack."

"Do you have any reason to think he would want to harm you?"

"No."

"I take it he was a bit of a joker."

"Oh yes," Maria said. "He had a mischievous sense of humor."

"Have you seen any of these apparitions of your father?" Kathleen asked Anne.

"No," Anne said. "But I desperately want to make contact with him."

"And why is that?" Kathleen said. It seemed to her everyone had an agenda when it came to the paranormal.

Anne paused and there was an uncomfortable silence in the room for a moment. "We had an argument before he died," she finally said. "I want to make things right with him."

Kathleen shifted the line of questioning to the little girl ghost and was questioning them on who she might be when Mark entered the living room. "Excuse me," he said. "Take a look at this."

By that time, Jacob and Angela had returned from the basement, where they had set up recording equipment. With Anne following, they walked into the hallway of the small renovated home and Mark pointed to some locks installed on the exterior of both bedroom doors. The hardware was designed to lock someone inside the bedrooms with a key. The locks could not be accessed from inside the rooms.

"There's another one like that in the basement bedroom," Jacob said.

"Did you put these locks on the door?" Mark asked.

"No," Anne said. "They were there when we bought the house five years ago."

"I think you should take them off," Kathleen said, wondering what kind of torment had been inflicted on the people who had been locked inside these rooms.

Anne nodded.

"Who owned the house before you?" Mark asked.

"I don't know," Anne said. "It was vacant, owned by a company. We bought it through our realtor, never looked into the history."

A few minutes later, Mark and Kathleen were in the basement of the house inspecting the guest bedroom where Anne claimed to have seen the ghost of the little girl a few times. Mark waved the EMF meter over the bed and the reading spiked. There were no electrical appliances or outlets of any kind nearby that might have caused it.

"Does anybody have a cell phone turned on?" Kathleen asked as Anne walked into the bedroom and noticed the high EMF reading. Cell phones would also skew EMF readings due to the electromagnetic energy they released.

Anne and Mark shook their heads and Kathleen ran the EMF meter over the bed again. The second time it registered nothing. They went through the entire house with cameras and EMF meters, occasionally calling out to the spirits to announce their presence.

Nothing noticeable occurred, and a few minutes later they had gathered in the basement living room, in the dark with only their flashlights. Kathleen held a video camera with a handheld tripod and had it pointed at a gas fireplace, which Anne had explained would occasionally turn on and off mysteriously during the day or in the middle of the night.

Mark would occasionally call out to the spirits, the little girl, or Anne's father, but they weren't getting any response, other than the odd flash of an EMF meter they had positioned on a coffee table in the middle of the room.

"If you are here, please make some noise to let us know," Mark said as they sat in the basement. Anne had by now joined the group while Maria sat upstairs, watching TV on the living room couch.

They waited and heard nothing. Then, suddenly, from the furnace room a knocking sound, hollow and wooden like someone banging on a door.

"If you're here please make the sound again," Mark said.

Silence.

Kathleen's video camera went dead. "Mark, my camera just shut off. Could you check the batteries?" He opened the battery case, reported they were fine and noticed the switch on the camera had been turned to the off position. "Did you do that?" he asked Kathleen.

"No," she said. Pointing to the tripod, "My hands were right here, nowhere near the power-switch." The digital thermometer registered a drop in temperature and Kathleen shivered.

"Maybe we should take a break," she said. They had been at it for two hours.

Upstairs in the kitchen they sat around chatting, drinking coffee and eating donuts that Anne had hospitably provided. By that time it was almost midnight. Maria had gone to bed, a digital recorder on her bedside table.

Anne's expression turned grim and she put her hands to her face. "I wanted to talk to my dad," she said, beginning to cry.

"Can't you guys get in touch with him? I want to say I'm sorry. I'm sorry, dad. If you're here, please forgive me. I didn't mean it. Please forgive me."

Kathleen put an arm on Anne's shoulder. "Anne, spirits don't always come out on demand, in spite of what you might see on TV shows. Sometimes, actually most of the time, we don't discover anything significant until we analyze the data."

Anne had stopped crying and was wiping her face with a tissue. "How long does that take?"

"With all the video cameras and recorders, sometimes weeks," Kathleen said. "But don't worry, we'll let you know when it's all done. We're also going to look into the history of your property, which we usually do anyway. Those locks bother me."

"You can talk to ghosts, right?" Anne asked.

"Sometimes I believe I can," Kathleen said, a grotesque image of Elizabeth Pelletier appearing in her mind. *I talk to ghosts all the time. I have one inside me right now. Would you like to meet her?*

"Could you please tell the little girl she's safe here, tell my dad I'm sorry for arguing with him?" Anne struggled to compose herself as the group tried not to stare at her.

Angela's face suddenly turned ashen-white.

"Are you okay?" Jacob said.

"Yeah," she said unconvincingly.

He led her outside for some fresh air.

Kathleen heard the door close behind them.

"Are they okay?" Anne asked.

For the first time Kathleen wasn't sure. She had felt a dark energy in the room moments before Angela had become pale.

Judging by Mark's somber expression, it looked like he had felt it too.

Kathleen cleared her throat. "Little girl, if you're here, please know that you are safe in this house. You can stay if you want but please behave yourself." She paused a moment before continuing. "Bruce, if you're here, you're welcome to stay as well. Your daughter loves you and she's sorry for arguing with you. Please forgive her."

Kathleen had said it more to please Anne than anything else. Her gut told her the dark energy did not come from Anne's father, whose presence she could not feel at all. Nor did it come from the little girl, whose presence was vaguely detectable. No, there was some other dark and evil force at work in this house that, within the last five minutes, had made itself apparent to Kathleen.

Elizabeth, where are you when I need you? Expel this evil presence, please.

A few minutes later, Jacob returned with Angela, claiming she wasn't well. "Would it be alright if we left?"

Mark nodded his agreement and Kathleen seconded it. After all, they had only brought the one vehicle. And PEIPI protocol specified if one wanted to go, they would all go. Besides it was coming up one in the morning and Kathleen still had to work tomorrow, as they all did.

There was an oppressive silence in Black Death a half hour later as Mark drove along the highway to Montague. The usual group dynamic—light conversation, joking, and laughter—had vanished.

Still pale, Angela stared out the window vacantly and Kathleen couldn't help but wonder what had happened to her friend in that house. Something evil had scared the shit out of her.

And Mark's vacant expression did not offer her much consolation.

Only Jacob seemed to be his normal, if concerned, self.

What the hell was happening to PEIPI? Kathleen didn't know. But, in the recesses of her troubled mind, she was going to find out and something told her it was going to be pretty fucking far from pretty.

Chapter Seven

"That's not pretty," forensics lab technician Stan Neiderman said, holding his nose and setting the decorative wine bottle recovered at Poverty Beach on a table, the following afternoon.

Detective Redmond backed away, not wanting to get anywhere near the oppressive odor. "It's pretty fucking far from pretty. But what's in it?"

Stan, a diminutive bald man, large horn-rimmed glasses framing his normally cheerful face, looked agitated. "Hang on," he snapped. He reached for a plastic bag, sealed the bottle in it, stepped back from the table and took a few deep breaths. After some time, his usual demeanor returned. "That shit makes your blood boil."

"I know," Redmond said. "Do you know the contents?"

"We've identified some components but not all." He picked up a clipboard and studied it. "There's a lot of alcohol in there. Uhhhm, bat's wing. Pepper. Some dirt. Some kind of animal fat. Water. Apple juice. Vanilla extract. Blood. And two unknown substances were still working on." He peeled off a carbon copy, handed it to Redmond. "You can keep that."

Redmond studied the lab report. "What do you make of it?"

"I've never come across anything like it before. It's some kind of potion I think. Have you ever smelled anything that makes you feel so agitated?"

The detective shook his head. "Any fingerprints?"

"We were able to pick up a partial print that I've run through the data base. No match yet, but were cross-referencing it now, so we still might get a hit."

"What about the bottle?"

"It was manufactured in Halifax in 1897. It's antique, probably worth some money. The name of the glass shop, long out of business, is in the report."

"Thanks," Redmond said, heading for the exit door. "Put the evidence in a safe place. And if you get anything else, let me know right away."

Stan nodded as the detective closed the door behind him.

A few minutes later, Redmond was cruising out of town to a job site he knew Mark was working today. He wanted to question him again about a possible description of the old lady. Jacob, Angela, and Kathleen had provided vague descriptions that resembled a third of the elderly female population in Montague and it was no help at all to the detective.

And he wasn't in a very good mood today.

Last night, he had forgotten to bring home dinner for his wife, Jeanette, and showed up drunk after polishing off more than a six-pack sitting alone in his car at Poverty Beach. She was none too pleased after he had staggered into bed well past midnight, put his arm around her lovingly and had tried to initiate sex.

Jeanette had pushed his hand away roughly, turned to him angrily and said "you're drunk" before storming out of the room, slamming the door behind her, and finding refuge for the night in their spare guest bedroom.

He had some ass-kissing to do if he was going to make things right again, otherwise he would be the one in the guest bedroom tonight.

He pulled into a small acreage a few minutes from town where Mark was loading debris into his black pick-up truck. The birds were singing, a gentle breeze blew and the sunlit sky was bright and cheery, quite the opposite of Redmond's mood.

Mark, who normally greeted the detective with a smile, only looked up curiously as he parked behind Black Death, stepped out and approached him.

"Can we talk for a few minutes?"

"Sure," Mark said, repositioning a piece of plywood he had just chucked in the back. He still had a white bandage supporting his reset nose, but eyeballed the detective like his nose was still out of joint.

"Can you shed any light on the description of the woman who kidnapped you, the location of the house, conversations with her, anything that might help me locate her?"

"I don't think so," Mark said, but then paused suddenly. *Help this man. He's your friend. Think.* His entire memory of the event had been erased, his only recollection of the old lady had come from information Kathleen had supplied last night, picking his brain for answers. He couldn't even remember attacking his friends with a flaming torch, never mind being kidnapped and held captive.

Redmond watched as Mark's eyes rolled back in his head, looking to the clear blue sky for answers. He didn't want to interrupt a man thinking, particularly when it might lead to the woman whom he knew with an eerie certainty was about to cut a swatch of bloodshed through the sleepy little town with her little potion of poison rage.

Mark's eyes cleared and he regarded Redmond. *Ruff, ruff. Barking.* "I think I heard a dog barking," he said. "And it sounded like a large dog."

"Anything else?"

"She had me in a dark place, a cellar accessed separately from the house."

"Any idea where this was?"

Mark shook his head. No matter how hard he tried, he could remember nothing else about the woman, his captivity, when or how he had been released.

After a few minutes of small talk, no more light was shed on the dark situation, so Redmond left.

Before getting in his car, he stopped. "If you remember anything, no matter how insignificant you think it is, call me. And I don't care what time of day or night it is, you call me. Got that?"

Mark nodded.

The detective closed the car door and pulled out of the driveway, scratching his head trying to remember how many old ladies owned large dogs and had homes with basements accessible either only or also from the exterior of the property.

Suddenly an image popped into his head and he veered off the highway onto a secondary road. *I think I know.*

Chapter Eight

"I think I know who that is," Kathleen told Jacob on the phone a few minutes later.

She was sitting at her computer, had just read an email, and called him immediately. It read:

> *Kathleen, if you can help me please do. Angela has been behaving very despondently lately and I'm getting worried about her and about our relationship. She reacted so strangely the other night I started investigating Anne's property immediately. Do you know who used to own it? Raymond Dodson. Do you know who that is? I think it's better if we discuss this over the phone or in person. Please call me when you receive this.*
>
> *Your friend, Jacob.*

"Do you?" Jacob asked.

"Isn't it her grandfather's brother?"

"Yeah, the oddball who she won't talk about. Did she ever mention him to you?"

"Just in passing. Something about him being the black sheep of the family."

"He's the black sheep alright."

"What do you mean?"

"I found an EVP on the digital recorder last night. Stayed up most of the night going over the data. You still remember what an EVP is?"

Is he taking a shot at me over my recent memory loss? Never mind. "Electronic Voice Phenomena refers to voices undetectable to the human ear but detectable by special recording equipment. You think I forgot our basic training?"

"No. Sorry. Do you know what I found?"

Kathleen felt a lump in her throat and swallowed hard. After her terrible day at work, she wasn't sure she wanted to know right now. Ron Baglund had chewed her ass out good right in front of two colleagues. "If you ever decide in your infinite wisdom that the straps I use to restrain these unruly kids are not right, or anything I'm doing here is not right, you make damned sure you come to me first, in person, not through email. And, if I ever find out you are going behind my back with these issues to the vice-principal or the principal, I will have your lily-white ass fired so fast it will make your dizzy little head spin."

Kathleen had felt her face redden during the tongue-lashing, and after work it was all she could do to rush out the exit door, run to a nearby park, sit down at a park bench and bawl her eyes out. At one time, prior to all the shit in her life, she had an idea how to handle Baglund. Give the control-freak control and he won't know what to do with it. Now, she was just afraid of him and tried to make sure she was never caught in the same room with him alone, for fear of a reprimand. She didn't know how much longer she could handle it and had started to think about other career opportunities. Surely something, anything, even working as a cashier at the local supermarket like Angela would be less stressful than dealing with Baglund.

Thank God Mark had not been home when she had arrived. She was in no mood to deal with the distance she had recently noticed that he was starting to put between their relationship, a crack that had started after he had been released from the hospital and had now widened into a fissure, soon to be a crevice at this pace.

"Kathleen, you there?"

"Yeah. Sorry. I drifted for a second."

"Well, don't you want to know what I found?"

"Go ahead."

"A male voice. Should I tell you or you want to hear the tape?"

Kathleen wanted to get it over with. *And I'm trying to get off my medication. Good timing, chick.*

"Just tell me."

"The voice says 'Leave this fucking house now bitch before I rape you again.'"

"Holy shit," Kathleen said.

"And the time of the EVP was around the time Angela turned white and left the house. There's something else," Jacob said. "I did some research at the library today. Guess what I found out?"

"Jacob, I had a shitty day today and I'm not in the mood for guessing."

"Sorry ... Raymond Dodson. He's dead now. But I found an old newspaper article about him. He was accused of being a pedophile. And he was accused of kidnapping a thirteen-year-old girl, Lila Parker, and locking her in a bedroom in the house where Maria lives now. Who knows what he might have done to her in there. He owned it then."

"What happened?"

"All the charges were dropped. None of the victims would talk and there wasn't enough evidence."

"And Lila Parker?"

"Found dead, washed up on the beach a few days after kidnapping charges against Raymond were dropped. Murder was suspected but never proven. No one was ever charged."

Kathleen paused while she connected the dots. *The little girl in the house is Lila Parker. Her restless soul is trapped there. The dark presence I felt is Raymond Dodson, Angela's great-uncle. 'Leave this house bitch before I rape you again.' Angela was raped by her great-uncle and these ugly scars have suddenly turned into gaping, infected wounds. No wonder she's fucked up.*

"How did Raymond Dodson die?" Kathleen asked.

"You're quick. I knew you would get to that. The obituary I found says he passed away quietly in his sleep while staying over at his brother Jim's house."

"That's it?"

"That's all I could find. Just the obituary. Apparently the death was never investigated."

"You know what this means?"

"I do. It means the psycho ghost that almost killed Angela is Raymond Dodson, her great-uncle. It also means he's probably still haunting his old house and her old house."

"Which means inhabitants of both properties are in danger."

"Not to mention my relationship," Jacob said. "What are we going to do?"

"Don't say anything to Angela. Until I talk to her. In the meantime, we have to think about getting into Maria's house again, and contacting the people who bought Angela's house. Where is Angela now?"

"She's at work."

"Okay, I'll talk to you later. I'm going to see her."

Kathleen scribbled a note for Mark, picked up her black cat Spike, planted a large kiss on her nose, gently put her on the couch and left. Spike meowed as she left in a tone demanding more affection. For a feral animal, she sure had become a big baby who needed her fair share of tender loving care. If she didn't get it, she'd be quick to let you know.

Twenty minutes later, Kathleen had parked in the Sobeys supermarket parking lot, barely able to get a spot, as Friday afternoons were always busy. She rushed inside and was now waving to Angela as she rang in a customer's grocery items.

Angela smiled as she recognized her friend, pointed to her watch and held up five fingers, indicating she would be off work at that time. Kathleen gestured with a hand, indicating she would wait for her outside in the parking lot and disappeared.

Seven minutes later, Angela walked out the door, this time a look of concern on her soft features. Her blue eyes were troubled. They hugged and Kathleen suggested they go to the nearby Montague Marina, where they could sit in the sun on a picnic table, sip coffee and watch the many boats anchored at the docks. It was a relaxing and pleasant place to hang out, a beautiful hot sunny day to boot.

Angela nodded and a few minutes later they were settled in with their coffees, sitting at a picnic table and watching absently as the captain of a fishing boat called *Delilah Blue* slowly drifted up to the dock, shouting for his shipmate to get the rope ready. A young lady pushed a crib along the concrete walking path in front of them, her infant son giggling up at her. The lush trees were visible on the far shore of Montague River.

The first few minutes were taken up by small talk and then Kathleen cut to the chase: "How are you, Angela? I mean, how are you really?"

"I got a bit freaked out the other night."

"I know. What happened?" Kathleen had a pretty good idea what happened but wanted to see if her friend would try putting up a smoke screen. They had become pretty close over the last few years, but she still suspected Angela had some skeletons in the closet. Who didn't? Kathleen had a sixth sense about these things.

Angela paused, searching her friend's eyes.

"The truth please," Kathleen said. "You want my help don't you?"

Angela nodded. "I thought I heard a voice say something nasty to me."

"What did it say?" *This isn't fair. I know already.*

There was another pause and Kathleen saw a lone tear form in Angela's left eye, drop and stream down her face. "If you don't want to talk about it now, you don't have to," Kathleen suddenly decided, now uncomfortable with Angela's pained expression.

Angela wiped her eyes. "It's okay. Maybe I should get it off my chest."

Kathleen put a maternal arm around her friend's shoulder. "I'm listening."

"You remember a few months back, when I was haunted by that ghost in my grandfather's house?"

"Yeah."

"Well, I wasn't completely honest with you guys. I suspected the ghost was Raymond Dodson, my great-uncle. But I didn't want to say anything. Anyway, I thought I had put the whole thing behind me but slowly thoughts of that fucking pervert have been creeping back in. Then, the other night when we pulled up to that house all the ugly memories flooded back. That was Raymond's house. Somewhere in the middle of the investigation, I thought I heard a voice ordering me out, threatening to rape me again if I didn't leave. Anyway, I got really upset and left."

Kathleen nodded and hugged Angela, who had started to cry softly. Kathleen produced a tissue and wiped Angela's face. She suspected there was more. "Is that it?"

There was a long pause.

"No ... If I tell you this you have to promise me you'll never tell anyone unless I give you permission to. I don't want this information in the wrong hands."

Kathleen braced herself for what she thought she was going to hear. "Done."

"When I was young, maybe nine or ten, I used to visit my grandfather, Jim, at the house I inherited. Jim was a great guy and we were really close. Anyway, one night when I was sleeping over his oddball brother Raymond shows up. Jim later went out somewhere and left me with him. That night Raymond raped me. I mean violently raped me. He told me if I told anyone he'd kill me, so I kept my mouth shut."

Kathleen nodded sympathetically while Angela continued. "Anyway, a week or two goes by, he shows up again and Jim isn't around. I don't know where he went but he stepped out somewhere. So her rapes me again, this time even more violent than the last. Well, a few hours later he goes to bed, I creep up to his bedroom while he's asleep and suffocate him to death with a pillow."

There was a long pause, the tears now running freely down her face. "I killed him Kathleen. I killed my uncle."

"Don't worry about it, sweetie. He was a demented pedophile according to Jacob. He deserved what he got. Think of all the other unsuspecting victims you might have saved."

Angela looked at her friend in shock. "Does Jacob know?"

"He doesn't know you killed him, will never know unless you decide to tell him. But he stayed up all night doing research, going through the data. He's pieced together all the rest, there's even an EVP of a male voice ordering you out of the house." Kathleen decided to leave the rape part out of it. She was sure her friend didn't need to hear the word again after what she'd been through. "Angela, he's trying to help you. He's worried about you."

They were silent for a few minutes, staring out at the collection of boats in the marina, oblivious to the glee-filled voices of children playing nearby.

"We're going back to Maria's house," Kathleen finally said. "That little girl was one of his victims. We need to get rid of that nasty apparition, condemn him to a life of suffering in hades if possible."

Angela smiled weakly.

"And we need to track down the new owners of your old home. They could be in danger. Do you know who they are?"

"I have a copy of the purchase contract," Angela said. "Their names are on it."

"Good. Get that to me please. The other thing, I don't think you should come. This is hitting way too close to home for you and you've been through enough."

Kathleen produced a business card. "It's my counselor. She's very good. I'd give her a call if I were you. There's no shame in trying to help yourself."

Chapter Nine

"Do you really think you can help yourself?" Beatrice Maling said, her ugly weathered face inches from Detective Redmond's defiant eyes.

He twisted in the ropes binding his arms, grunted, and spit in her face. He had just woken up.

She recoiled, slapped him in the face and limped over to the black magic table.

Maybe she was right. But he wasn't going down without a fight. In exactly the same spot Mark Riley had wound up only a few short days ago, the detective silently chastised himself for being so stupid. He had let his guard down. He had arrived at this old bat's house drunk.

After checking four or five properties earlier in the day, he had been wrong about his initial instincts, he finally remembered the shopping-cart lady. Going by the name Bertha, he doubted that was her real name now. She had always been an odd duck.

Russ Willard, one of his colleagues, had once relayed a story to him about Bertha, saying he had tried to get her to shove along after loitering for a number of hours in Sobeys parking lot and she had gone ballistic on him, swearing and cursing, throwing out the one-finger salute and telling him in no uncertain terms to "watch your fucking manners young man if you know what's good for you."

After draining eight beers, Redmond had pulled up to her secluded oceanfront acreage at dusk. A pit bull guarded the premises, along with a young heavy-set man with wild hair, wilder eyes, and greasy coveralls. He appeared to be mentally deficient. She had called him Bob.

The man had slipped into the barn with a rake as he noticed Redmond pull in. Thinking back now, that should have been his first clue that something wasn't right. But, in an alcoholic haze, he had knocked on the door of the old house, made some initial inquiries and the old bag had invited him in for tea, which he had erroneously accepted. Of course it had been spiked with a powerful chemical that had knocked him out. How could he have been so daft? Trust your gut. But it's not an easy thing to do when your judgment is impaired by booze.

Now, here he was, stripped down to his underwear, securely tied down in a fowl-smelling dark cellar and forced to listen to this lunatic's bullshit. *Humor her, Blaine. Calm down. Find out what she wants.*

"What's your real name, Bertha? You do want me to call you by your real name, don't you?"

She turned around from the table, her face faintly illuminated by a candle's small yellow flame. She smiled a crooked smile, exposing rotten teeth. "If I tell you, I'll have to kill you ... but I guess it doesn't matter ... I'm going to kill you anyway."

She found this humorous and burst into an odd giddy laugh. "I'm really Beatrice Maling. But I changed my name a long time ago to Bertha Mooney, to fool idiots like you."

"So you're a descendent of James Maling."

"My great-grandfather. And what a splendid man he was."

"So that's what this is about. Revenge."

"You guessed it, Sherlock. I guess that's why you're a detective and not a beat cop like your other flunkies. You condemned the revered reverend to a life in hell. Now that's where you'll end up."

"What's your end game?"

"You're not going to be around long enough to find out."

"Then what's the harm in telling me?"

She considered this for a moment while mixing up a potion. "Let's just say that when I'm done this town will understand why they should have listened to James a hundred years ago."

Her eyes went far away and she started murmuring something. A spell. She was casting a spell. A minute or so later, holding up the potion to her face, she limped toward the detective, the vial in one hand, a large dagger in the other.

"You have a choice," she said. "Drink the potion," waving the dagger in front of him, "or I cut out your heart."

Chapter Ten

"If your heart's not in it, don't go," Kathleen said to Mark as she prepared to leave that evening for Maria's house in an attempt to rid the haunted property of the evil apparition occupying it.

Mark had been despondent after she had arrived home from her conversation with Angela, and had sat on the couch silently channel-surfing. Kathleen had no idea what had gotten into him and she didn't have time to find out. She was worried about Anne and Maria and the new owners of Angela's house, Burke and Samantha Stone. Perhaps more importantly, or at least equally important, they had a thirteen-year-old daughter, Paige, who had recently been complaining of difficulty sleeping and the sense of an eerie presence in her bedroom at night. As well, the child's behavior had started to become erratic. It seemed she had started acting out and rebelling against her parents within the last two weeks.

Kathleen had promised Anne they would be at her house tonight, and she had also told Samantha that, if time permitted, the team would also come by her house later that evening.

Angela would of course be absent from what could turn into a double paranormal investigation in the course of one night, but Jacob was on his way over now.

Mark stared at her blankly as she loaded gear into a duffle bag. Spike was huddled underneath the TV stand making a sporadic and eerie hissing sound. If the cat could talk, she would probably warn Kathleen of the dangers ahead. But, since she couldn't, she only hissed, forecasting danger in the only way she knew how.

"Well?" Kathleen tried to read his mind. Lately she wasn't able to, as his expression was mostly blank.

He looked up at her, a dim semblance of reality registering. This was not the Mark Kathleen had come to know and love.

"I think I'll pass," he said glumly. "Sorry."

She kissed him perfunctorily on the cheek, grabbed the duffle bag and left. As she closed the door, Spike meowed loudly and darted into the kitchen. It was not her vying-for-attention meow. Kathleen knew that much about her cat.

A few minutes later they pulled up to Maria's house in Black Death. They were quiet on the trip. Kathleen was wrestling with something she thought she had forgotten and as they pulled into the long and winding driveway she remembered. *Detective Redmond. He said he was going to call me today and he didn't. That's not like him.*

She thought of calling the detective as they walked up the small porch, but then realized it probably wasn't a good idea right now. PEIPI had strict confidentiality protocol concerning paranormal investigations and she wasn't about to breach that by calling Redmond. He would surely ask where she was and she didn't want to lie. They had become good friends after their dramatic near-death ordeal a few months back, and Kathleen was in no mood to start infusing a bunch of lies into a relationship she thought would be much better served by telling the truth. No. Better not call. It would have to wait until tomorrow.

She felt it as soon as she entered the house. The dark presence was there and it immediately chilled her body. They had decided earlier the basement was the best place to set up, so she pushed through the evil force, fighting to control panic rising up in her throat, carried the duffle bag into the basement, and began unloading some gear.

Jacob was right behind her.

This wasn't a typical paranormal investigation. They did not plan on putting recording equipment in every room. Kathleen wanted to contact Raymond Dodson, lay his spirit to rest and assure the little girl (whom she was sure was Lila) that she could stay in safety or move on with her family.

Of course, it sounded easy. But that's rarely how it worked.

Anne's mother Maria had left for the evening. Anne had made arrangements for her to spend the night in Montague. They didn't feel her fragile mind could cope with the violence that might accompany an attempt to send an evil bastard on his way to hell. But Anne had decided to stay. She was upstairs in the living room now, watching TV, waiting for Kathleen's signal to come down.

Kathleen wondered as she set up a video camera if it was also Raymond who had been assaulting Paige, the little girl in Angela's former property. If that were the case, it meant this spirit moved around between different properties. She had no idea if he had a few other stops on his route that might require her talents. Or the talents of Elizabeth Pelletier, who she hoped she could rely on.

Liz, you in there? I may need you out here.

Anne and Jacob joined Kathleen in the lower living room after turning out the lights.

"Do you feel anything?" Anne asked, looking at Kathleen through the still light of the moon, shining through the basement window. Anne had her left hand bandaged. She'd suffered a nasty cut that required stitches, after removing the three exterior locks on all bedroom doors. It seemed someone didn't want those locks removed.

"I did when I came in. But nothing yet."

Jacob clicked on a recorder and they sat in silence for a few minutes, listening for sounds, monitoring temperature and electromagnetic energy. The EMF meter sat on the coffee table in the middle of the room. It seemed like a good place for it, giving everyone a good view of the small LED lights that would illuminate and register significant changes in energy levels.

Kathleen was hoping to get this over with in a hurry. Prior to leaving, she had popped two anti-anxiety pills and now it seemed, a few days after wanting to get off the pills completely, she wasn't even monitoring her intake anymore.

What she found particularly disturbing was Mark's change in attitude. She had never seen apathy like that from him before and it worried her. Normally, it would be unheard-of for him to not accompany them on an investigation—he would worry too much about Kathleen's safety. He was the leader after all, and they would usually hand the floor to him when it came to actually contacting the spirits. With all his experience, he just seemed to know what to say.

And not having him here had left her with a vacancy in her heart and mind. She missed him, and the pangs of emotion that go with missing someone were tweaking at her now, creating confusion and an inability to focus. She was sure the medication was adding to the fog. *How could you live with someone and miss them at the same time?*

"Are you going to say something or you want me to?" Jacob asked.

Kathleen realized she had been staring blankly for the last few minutes, unaware two people were watching her, waiting for her to proceed. *Snap out of it girl. These people need you here.*

"I'll carry on," she said. "Sorry."

Kathleen jumped as a thumping sound was heard in the furnace room, the same hollow knocking they'd heard a few days earlier.

"Raymond Dodson, we know who you are," Kathleen said. "And I'm here to say your reign of terror is over. It's time for you to leave this house forever. Leave these people alone."

They waited.

Silence.

Then the knocking again in the furnace room, and a crashing sound. Something had fallen over. Jacob, flashlight beam guiding his way, jumped up and ran into the furnace room. A cardboard box with an artificial Christmas tree had been tipped off a storage shelf, along with a box containing glass canning jars. A few of the canning jars had fallen out of the box and shattered on the concrete floor, and a few Christmas tree branches poked from the box, pointing eerily at the shattered jars.

Jacob and Kathleen stared at the mess and Anne crept up behind them.

"Do you want me to clean it up?" she said.

"No," Kathleen instructed. "Leave it for now."

"I'm in you and you're in me."

Well, if that's the case I need you now.

Jacob noticed it first and then Anne. They both looked horrified. Kathleen's demeanor had suddenly changed, her facial features transforming into someone else entirely. Even her posture was different. She looked serious, focused, the opposite of her expression five seconds ago.

"Evil will not be tolerated in this house," Elizabeth said, wandering through the finished basement and into the bedroom where Lila had been spotted. Elizabeth sat on the bed. "You will never lay a hand on little Lila ever again in your life."

When they discussed it later, Anne and Jacob both admitted to feeling a dark and cold presence go right through them before the carnage started, a feeling that would haunt them for years to come. They also admitted to hearing a guttural growling sound, like the warning sound a wolf makes before attacking its prey.

Then all hell broke loose.

The guttural growl was accompanied by words, incomprehensible at first, but as the apparition of Raymond Dodson stormed into the bedroom and grabbed Elizabeth by the neck, the words became recognizable.

"Die, you fucking bitch, die," he said as he slammed her into the bedroom wall, knocking over a bedside lamp that shattered with a pop.

Jacob was yelling something, Anne behind him yelling something else as Kathleen's face turned purple, her eyes bulging in their sockets. But her expression belied the imminent danger she was in.

She stoically stared at her attacker and smiled.

Then something strange happened. At the same time as Kathleen's body withered to the floor, coughing, gasping for breath, the spirit of Elizabeth Pelletier exited. And, unlike her previous appearance when she had looked bruised, slashed, battered, head smashed in, with one eye dangling precariously from an eye socket, her thin nightgown covered in blood, this time her spirit looked absolutely radiant and angelic.

She had flowing long brown hair, a simple black dress, a focus and intensity in her eyes that warned a person she was not one to mess with.

While Jacob ran to the aid of Kathleen, Liz battled with the ghost of Raymond. The energy generated by the fight was enormous. Both combatants swirled around the room, bouncing off walls, pulling hair, punching, choking, mixed in with pain-filled shouts, some decipherable, some gobbledygook.

It was a luminescent grey mass, a cyclonic force, whipping around the room, spinning high winds, debris, and a chill that Jacob had never felt the likes of in his entire life.

A hurricane of paranormal proportion.

Anne's eyes had widened in horror, fleeing up the stairs and out of the house, where she stood now, taking deep breaths, trying to calm her frenetic heart. She was frozen in fear, unable to enter her mother's house even if she wanted to.

Jacob picked Kathleen up and escorted her away from the storm. He plopped her down on the living room couch while she gasped for breath, her expression slowly returning to something approximating normal. This was his friend Kathleen again, he could tell from the familiar brown eyes and attractive face.

The small basement window shattered, the glass becoming airborne, getting caught up in the swirling, furious pace of the raging battle inside the small room.

Then as quickly as the fury erupted, the small bedroom became quiet, the howling wind slowly subsiding, small previously airborne objects dropping to the floor with clunking sounds.

Clunk ... clunk ... clunk, then nothing at all.

"Are you okay?" Jacob asked, searching Kathleen's eyes.

"I am," she said, a half smile slowly emerging. "I think we got him."

"Let's hope," Jacob said, running up the stairs, outside onto the porch, where he comforted Anne, who hugged him tightly, unable to stop the tears pouring down, soaking Jacob's shoulder.

"Okay," he said gently. "I think it's over."

He finally coaxed her back inside the house. They walked downstairs, Jacob calling out Kathleen's name as they descended. Their eyes widened for a second time, but this time not in fear, as they peered in the bedroom and saw Kathleen.

"It's over now," Kathleen said to the small apparition of Lila Parker. She sat on the bed, strewn with debris and glass, and the little girl, blonde pony tails, bright blue eyes, freckles, wearing a white dress with red and yellow flowers, stood in front of Kathleen, her arm outstretched, offering a gift.

In her hand was a bouquet of red roses. Kathleen took them and held them to her bosom as she gently stroked the smiling girl's hair. "You're free to return to your family or stay here as long as you behave yourself."

Lila looked at Anne and said, "I'm sorry."

Then she floated into the air, hovered momentarily, and disappeared through the bedroom ceiling.

Kathleen, examining the roses with disbelief, couldn't understand how she was still able to hold them in her hand. It defied all the laws, definitions and rules of paranormal investigation, that the ghost of a small girl would be able to produce a bouquet of roses out of thin air, disappear, and the roses would remain.

But Kathleen wasn't in the mindset to begin questioning anything right now. She worried that the ghost of Raymond Dodson had not passed on to the other side—wherever that was. Maybe he had just relocated to the very same residence he had raped and almost killed Angela Dodson.

There was another small girl—this one very much alive—who was potentially in grave danger.

Reading Kathleen's concerned expression, Jacob immediately started packing up the gear. Kathleen handed the flowers to Anne, hugged her, and began helping him. Anne had calmed down by now and thanked them profusely as they packed their belongings into Black Death.

Chapter Eleven

Black Death pulled onto the quiet residential street where the Stones lived. It was dead quiet. Kathleen had called while en route, Jacob navigating the easy fifteen-minute drive. In a tense voice, Samantha had said Paige, her thirteen-year-old daughter, had barricaded herself in her bedroom, refusing to come out. As well, the teenager was uttering profanities and throwing things at the bedroom door, wanting everyone to leave her "the hell alone and stay the fuck out of my life."

Thinking it may be a good time for police involvement, PEIPI certainly wasn't authorized to handle unruly teens, particularly if they didn't want to leave their bedrooms, Kathleen had checked the time, a quarter to midnight, and decided to call Detective Redmond. Hadn't the detective told her to call him any time of day or night if she was in danger? She was pretty sure he had. And, if he hadn't, she was pretty sure he would forgive her.

But the detective's phone had gone to voice mail without even ringing. She found that strange. As long as she'd known him, he rarely turned the phone off, particularly at night, when he might receive a hot tip on one of his cases that could very well go cold the next morning if he wasn't immediately available. That's how police work was at times. If you weren't available to receive the lead, sometimes it ended up in never-never land.

Where the hell is he?

She put the thought out of her mind as she looked at Jacob, who was staring at her. "You up for this?" she said.

"I am. You're the one who's been through a shit-storm lately. Are you up for it?"

Kathleen sighed. "Do we have a choice?"

It was a rhetorical question so they simultaneously exited the vehicle, each carrying gear.

Samantha and Burke, a young couple in their late twenties, were standing at the door waiting, peering out the small window as they walked up the small path to the house.

The Stones had been briefed on who might be terrorizing their daughter.

Samantha, pale and nervous, opened the door and greeted them. Kathleen forced her most-confident smile and they walked into the living room and sat down. Jacob and Burke made small talk while Samantha offered them drinks.

Kathleen and Jacob shook their heads. They wanted to discuss the worsening situation.

The bedroom door, the former bedroom of her friend Angela, thudded as objects bounced off it, every so often followed by "fuck off ... get the fuck out of here ... leave me the fuck alone" and at one point Kathleen distinctly heard "fuck this, fuck that, and fuck you!"

This certainly was not good. Not good at all. As she sat in the living room, thinking of the horrific incidents that had taken place here when Angela had been raped and almost murdered, even sexually assaulted by a ghost, the awful memories flooding back into her mind, Kathleen came to a sudden realization. She had no idea what to do. She wasn't prepared to deal with the possible possession of a tender-aged teenager like Paige.

And what were the possible ramifications if she mishandled the situation? She didn't even know these people—didn't know them from Adam and Eve. They could turn around and blame her if something went wrong, even charge her with something in this day and age. Was it worth the risk?

Then a horrific shriek of pain that echoed from behind the door of the small bedroom decided it for her in an instant.

There was a girl in need of help here. If she was worried about legal ramifications she should never have signed on for this job in the first place. It was a little too late to start worrying about protocol, legal ramifications, liability issues and all that crap.

Liz, if you're around, I could really use your help about now. Maybe I said some bad things about you, to you before, but I take them all back now. Help me ... please!

Kathleen rose, waving her hand to the others to remain seated, and approached the door. "Listen Raymond, if you're in there, why don't you pick on someone your own size, instead of a thirteen-year-old girl. You degenerate piece of shit!!"

The bedroom suddenly became quiet. Kathleen approached the door, tried the handle. It was locked. "Paige, can you hear me?"

Soft sobbing sounds could be heard.

The maternal instincts of Samantha became overwhelming and she was about to stand. Kathleen waved her down and she sat obediently.

Jacob stood poised, like a swat team member without the assault rifle.

Burke, white-faced, looked like he might make a run for the door. This haunted shit wasn't for everybody. Many people thought they had the stomach for it. But when it came right down to it, it scared the hell out of most people.

Kathleen began again. "Paige, can you hear me? Open the door please. I'm here to help you."

The sobbing stopped suddenly and there was an eerie silence.

Then a gruff male voice: "Get the fuck out of here and leave me alone." It was the voice of Raymond Dodson.

My God. He's trying to possess that poor girl. If he hasn't already. Kathleen had had enough. She motioned to Jacob, who stood up with the duffle bag. "You got that hammer?" she said.

Jacob nodded and produced it. Along with recording equipment, they regularly conducted paranormal investigations with a few choice weapons. You just never knew when they might come in handy.

Kathleen looked at the Stones, who were not exactly displaying the collective image of the rock. Oh well, it was just a name anyway.

"Do you mind if I wreck this door?" Kathleen said. "And I'm not offering to pay for it."

Samantha and Burke nodded, almost in unison, and Kathleen nodded to Jacob, who began smashing the wooden door to pieces with the large hammer, not quite large enough to be called a sledgehammer, but certainly larger than your typical carpenter's hammer. Mark would know what to call it but Kathleen didn't have a clue, not that she cared anyway.

A few seconds later Jacob kicked open the door. The room was pitch-black, so Kathleen produced a flashlight, shining it around, trying to locate Paige. The room was absolute carnage. The bed had been tipped over, two bedside lamps shattered, a book case knocked over, large fist holes in the drywall, stuffed animals ripped open, stuffing strewn around the room.

But where was Paige?

She heard a squeak, raised the flashlight and her jaw dropped, not for the first time and certainly not for the last. The little girl, her brown hair disheveled, was pinned to the wall, her head touching the ceiling. Her white nightgown was ripped and barely clung to her small frame. Her eyes were wide with fear and her face turned purple as the life drained from her body. She was being choked to death.

It was Jacob who reacted first. As the Stones rushed to the bedroom doorway, screaming in panic, staring in shock and horror at their little girl being choked to death, Jacob sprang up on the overturned mattress, grabbed Paige's leg and pulled. He tugged hard on her leg for a moment, before she began to slide down the wall.

As she fell, the sinister spirit of Raymond Dodson appeared, his eyes red with rage, mouth agape with evil intentions, scooped up Jacob and flung him out the bedroom door. Kathleen ducked as the body flew passed her. Samantha and Burke weren't so fortunate. They were both knocked sideways as he flew passed them, slammed into the living room wall and melted down it, dazed but not unconscious.

Raymond was on Jacob in a hurry. He picked him up, slammed his head into the drywall a few times and started choking him, his method of choice for murder.

By this time, Samantha and Burke were attending to their crying daughter who was looking at them dazed and confused.

Kathleen ran into the living room and frantically pulled at Jacob's arm, trying to release him from the death grip.

Then it happened. Liz floated into the room, same black dress, same confident and focused demeanor. "Let him go now!" she demanded.

Jacob fell to the floor, coughing, images of Angela dancing in his head. This spot was exactly where he had rescued her.

Kathleen helped Jacob to his feet, walking him slowly to what she hoped was a safe corner as the spirits battled. It was not so much a whirlwind of activity this time as it was a display of Liz delivering a slow and methodical shit-kicking to the malicious spirit that once was a malicious man.

He grunted and groaned as she knocked him around the room with well-placed punches and kicks. This woman knew how to fight. Midway through, Raymond seemed to get a second wind and landed a kick that sent Liz sprawling across the room, her head thudding into the wall as she skidded into it.

Was that even possible? That the head of a ghost could thud against a wall, instead of going right through it? Well, if they could knock on walls, couldn't their heads also crash into them? But, Kathleen knew it wouldn't make any sense to even try to apply any laws of science to what they were witnessing right now. And she also knew that very few people would believe her story if she decided to repeat it. Perhaps only those who had had experiences with PEIPI would be more prone to accept the tales she could tell. After all they did more than hunt ghosts. Hell, they seemed to attract them at every turn.

Liz now seemed to be getting the better of her foe. She picked him up by the throat, elevated him in the air and smiled down at her guests. His head hung at an odd angle, his tongue dangling out of his mouth.

"He's ready for his trip to hades," she said, as they floated up and disappeared through the ceiling.

Samantha and Burke had hung back during the fight, attending to Paige, who had no memory of her violent past. They sat on either side of her, arms outstretched and wrapped around her shoulder, as Paige wiped away tears and surveyed the carnage that was once the very organized bedroom of a well-behaved teenager.

A few minutes later, Jacob and Kathleen were packed up and ready to leave, Jacob with a few more aches and pains in his body than when he had arrived. The couple thanked them and walked them to the front door, while their daughter, who had changed and cleaned herself up, sat on the couch staring at the TV in bewilderment. She would probably never know just how close she had come to death.

"Are you religious?" Kathleen asked as they stood on the porch about to depart.

"Yes," Samantha said.

"You may want to have your priest bless this house. And bless your daughter while he's at it."

As she threw the duffle bag into the truck bed of Black Death, Samantha, who was watching them from the doorway, opened the screen door and said: "I thought the realtor said that Casper the friendly ghost lives here?"

"I guess he moved out," Kathleen said, and climbed in the truck.

"How are you doing?" Kathleen said as they started the drive home. She had taken the wheel this time, noticing how badly Jacob was limping as they left. They both had red welts across their necks and a few aches and pains. Jacob had faired a little worse for wear. "Any serious injuries, you think?"

"I'll live," Jacob said. "I'll be fine. I'm young and I heal fast. And you?"

"Neck's a little sore, but otherwise right as rain."

"And mentally?"

"Let's not go there?"

"Probably not a good idea."

Chapter Twelve

Probably not a good idea, Kathleen decided when the thought of waking her passed-out boyfriend entered her mind. *Better to let him sleep it off, have it out with him tomorrow.*

She knew something was strange as soon as she got home. Spike normally greeted her at the front door and the cat was nowhere to be found. And the smell. The home reeked of beer and cigars, although she had never known Mark to be a smoker.

She had walked into the living room and found him snoring loudly on the black leather couch, legs dangling close to the floor. An ashtray overflowed with Colts Mild cigar butts, the coffee table was full of beer cans, a few scattered haphazardly on the floor. A can that had once been full had been knocked over and its contents spilled out into a pool of beer. A small rivulet snaked its way to her feet as she stood surveying the party scene. A thin cloud of pale blue smoke still hung in the air and she shook her head, opening a window to air the place out.

Meat Loaf's *Bat Out of Hell* blared on the stereo. Kathleen turned it off and walked into the kitchen calling Spike. Where was she? She flicked the kitchen light on and, noticing a mess of dishes piled high in the sink, frowned.

"Spike, sweetie, where are you?"

Silence, but for the faint, loud and labored snoring of Mark in the living room. She opened a few lower cabinets and finally saw her, huddled in a corner beside the garbage can below the sink. Spike was adept at opening and closing doors and sometimes when she was scared she would open the lower cabinet, crawl in and hide beside the garbage can, her favorite place of refuge. There were also a few holes in the wood near the back of the plumbing and Spike had trapped, toyed with and tortured, and finally killed a few mice there. Either she was hiding in fear or she was on nightshift sentry duty. But judging by her defensive stance, it appeared something had scared the little black cat. But since she had grown up as a feral animal in the forest before being domesticated, it didn't take much to scare the intelligent little creature. Kathleen could only imagine what kind of hardships and battles with other predators Spike had endured prior to becoming domesticated.

"Come on, Spike," Kathleen said, extending a hand inside the small dark space. Spike hissed, but it only made Kathleen laugh. Learned by surviving in the wild, this was a defense mechanism she did not think Spike would ever outgrow. Spike's first thought would always be that people were out to get her. If you wanted her trust, you had to earn it.

Kathleen waited and soon heard the loud motorized purring of Spike, in symphony with the snores echoing from the living room. She picked her up and Spike meowed loudly, a give-me more-attention-please meow.

She carried her into the bedroom, set her on the bed and changed into a pair of shorts and a pink t-shirt. She fluffed up a few pillows, pulled the purring cat closer, snuggled up with her in a fetal position, and yawned.

She was exhausted, physically and mentally drained from the evening's traumatic events. This ghost hunting was starting to take its toll and she didn't know how long she would be able to carry on. She sighed, turning her thoughts to more domestic chores. She had a massive house clean-up tomorrow and wasn't looking forward to it.

It was evening and she was in the old, but partially refurbished, two-story house she had only recently bought and moved into with Mark. She cleaned up the dishes by hand, placing a few with less stubborn stains into the dishwasher. She finished with the dishes, looked around the counter tops. They were still cluttered with junk, collectibles she had brought over when she moved from her small rented apartment. She started picking them up, carrying them to a kitchen pantry. She put in piece by piece, mixing dishes, plates, small appliances with food items and not caring one iota. She just wanted a clutter-free house.

Soon the pantry was overflowing and she picked up a flashlight and started carrying items out to the garage. But on her third trip she discovered to her horror the garage was stuffed and stacked floor-to-ceiling with junk. There was no room for more.

She grimaced, walked back into the kitchen. She frowned, looking at the kitchen counter. Had she made a dent? It didn't look like it. She hastily grabbed a few more small appliances, wondering as she walked into the basement why she needed three toasters anyway. She turned on the light, slowly made her way down the stairs. The basement was pretty full with junk already. *Cluttered house, cluttered mind.* Three trips later, she noticed, again to her horror, the basement was stuffed full of junk and she could barely move. For a minute she struggled, becoming trapped and tangled in the mound of debris. Finally freeing herself, she disgustedly turned off the light while returning to the kitchen.

She surveyed the kitchen counter. *What!!! More junk than when I started.*

She shook her head and walked into the living room, calling out to Mark. Her eyes widened in shock as she entered the room. It was overrun with garbage, old furniture, appliances, a treasure trove—if you were a hoarder. Mark was nowhere to be found.

I'm getting out of here. I need to clear my head. In retrospect Kathleen thought she could have taken the back door, it was less cluttered and at least she had an unobstructed path to the exit.

But instead, she started climbing the mound of debris littering the living room, consuming it really. Her pink t-shirt got snagged on an upturned chair at the top of the heap. When she turned around to pull the shirt free, her left foot sank, becoming tangled in a mass of barbed wire. She jerked it but the barbs only dug into her skin and tiny rivers of blood began to flow from the multiple cuts.

She tried to move her right leg but it burst through a cardboard box, becoming lodged in the gooey contents. Suddenly feeling the adrenaline of panic coursing through her veins, she tried to stand but sank to her knees, trapped in a quicksand pile of garbage.

She opened her mouth to scream but no words came out. *Cluttered house, cluttered mind. Good luck with that.*

Now in full panic mode, she wildly thrashed her arms, the movements becoming more restricted with each futile flailing motion.

Soon she couldn't move at all and had sunk to her neck. Horror-stricken, she realized the debris pile was very close to claiming her life. She opened her mouth, had to force the single word out with what little strength she had remaining: "Maaaaaaarrrk!"

"I'm here, honey," he said.

Drenched in sweat, she looked up at the concerned expression on her boyfriend's face, gripping her shoulders tightly in both hands. She blinked a few times, slowly waking up. *It was a nightmare, that's all. Get a grip.*

She looked around the room, noticing most of the blankets had disappeared from the bed, Spike long gone.

She was about to start rushing around preparing for work, but then realized it was Saturday and she had the weekend off. By that time Mark had taken his hands off her and sat on the bed. He wore a guilty expression.

"Sorry about last night," he said. "I've cleaned most of it up."

"It's okay." But it was pretty far from okay. It was a sign, and not the first, of a change in her boyfriend that she didn't like very much. "Do you have to work today?"

"Not until much later."

Good. It would give her time for a much-needed heart-to-heart with this man sitting next to her who now seemed like something marginally less than a complete stranger.

Mark rose from the bed. He looked confused. "I'll make breakfast," he said, leaving.

Kathleen nodded and glanced at the clock as she walked into the shower: 12:46 pm. Wow! She had slept in big time.

Sometime later, after eating bacon, eggs, sour-dough toast with strawberry jam, and orange juice, they sat around the living room, drinking coffee. Over breakfast Kathleen had briefed Mark on the two paranormal investigations last night and he had digested the information and nodded, giving her a strange look as though there was another, far more dangerous one yet to come. She could just read it in his face. She was good at that, reading people's intentions on their facial expressions. It went some way to explaining why everyone thought she was the best clairvoyant in the little province right now, a label she didn't necessarily like but was now starting to reluctantly accept.

She didn't like being in the limelight, but her investigations with PEIPI were slowly but surely placing her squarely in its scrutinizing glare.

After some small talk about their plans, Mark had to haul some debris in a few hours for a customer in neighboring Georgetown, and Kathleen planned a visit to the local police station to inquire on the whereabouts of Detective Redmond, Kathleen got to the point.

"What's wrong with you, Mark? You haven't been the same since your kidnapping." She decided not to bother mentioning the alcohol and cigar blow-out last night. His ordeal must have been traumatic, whatever it was, and she was willing to allow him to blow off a little steam—as long as it didn't turn into an addiction.

He paused, fidgeting with his hands, a habit he never had before. "I don't know. Since Redmond found me on the beach my life hasn't been the same. I feel this weird sense of foreboding, like something real ugly is about to happen."

"Well why don't you face it head-on, like you've always done before, instead of retreating into this shell? I've been starting to think something's wrong with me."

"Nothing's wrong with you," he said quickly. On the contrary, Kathleen realized there was a lot wrong with her right now, but she wasn't prepared to argue that point. Take your blessings when they come—they may be few and far between.

"Mark, we've always talked about our problems, for as long as I've been with you. Now, you're withdrawing, cutting me off, and I don't know how to handle it."

He stared at her. In his eyes, she could see a vague confusion, but also the innocence and honesty that had first endeared her to him.

He scratched his head as Spike entered the room, meowed and jumped on Kathleen's lap, instantly curling into a little ball and purring.

"Okay," he said. "I'll tell you what's on my mind."

"I wish you would."

He brought her up to speed on his conversation with Detective Redmond, telling her what he had said regarding the dark cellar, barking dog, and old lady. Then he paused for a moment before adding: "But lately I've been getting other fleeting memories of my abduction. I would have come with you last night but somehow, and I can't explain it in any rational way, it feels like if I'm there, I'm going to jinx you in some way and be responsible for harming you. And I don't want to do that Kathleen. You're the most important thing in my life. How could I live with myself if I came along on an investigation and something terrible happened to you? I wouldn't want to go on."

It was a difficult question but Kathleen had to ask. "Are you possessed?"

"No, it doesn't feel like it anyway."

"What does it feel like?"

"Like I'm under some kind of spell or something, to lead you into a trap ... I don't know."

"What sort of other memories are you getting of your abduction?"

"You remember how weird you say I was acting when we were celebrating Canada Day, after drinking that moonshine?"

"Yeah."

"Well, that scared the shit out of me ... that I could go after my best friends, even you." He paused a moment, trying to focus his thoughts. "It seems to me I drank something when I was kidnapped—threatened into drinking something."

"What kind of threat?"

He paused.

Kathleen knew he was thinking of a way to put it gently. "Just tell me, Mark."

"The woman said if I didn't drink it she would kill you."

"Kill me? How?"

"That's the unclear part. I don't remember. But I do remember another thing ... she said if I talk about this she will kill me and all PEIPI members. So you see why I didn't want to tell you?"

Kathleen was starting to understand. She also knew the disappearance of Detective Redmond was linked to this evil woman, whoever she was. It wasn't like Redmond to not answer his phone. She had called twice and no response. Her gut told her he was in terrible danger. And he wasn't the only one. If she didn't do something soon, this strung-out group of paranormal investigators could be lined up beside each other in a nearby cemetery six feet on the dark side of the dirt.

That was not a pleasant thought. She wasn't yet prepared for a subterranean home away from home.

Chapter Thirteen

"He's not at home, we know that for a fact," Police Constable Russ Willard told Kathleen as she stood at the front desk of the Montague police detachment that overcast Saturday afternoon. "His wife's in an absolute panic, been calling every hour, and several cars are out looking for him."

She already knew Redmond wasn't at home, but humored the young police officer, who was concerned for Redmond, a man he looked up to, respected, and viewed as a local hero.

Willard was twenty-eight, his brown hair cropped short in a brush cut. He also sported a goatee. He had friendly brown eyes and a cheerful disposition. Her gut told her she could trust him. "Maybe I could shed some light on this?"

Willard was no stranger to the rumors surrounding Kathleen's talents, and his eyebrows lifted at the suggestion. "Please, tell me what you know."

Kathleen reviewed the date of the detective's disappearance, how it happened just after his conversation with Mark, during which he had provided some important details of the woman, previously unknown to police. "Mark also told Redmond the old woman had a dog, a large one by the sound of it, and that he'd been held captive in a dark cellar with at least one entrance from the exterior of the house. That would have been enough for Redmond to wrack his brain and start pursuing some possible suspects. I'm sure he was looking for the old woman when he disappeared. And there's a good possibility she's holding him captive."

Willard scratched his goatee and pondered the information. "Problem is, he never called in his last location to the office, or informed us he was pursuing this new information. We weren't even aware he had started this investigation."

"Yeah but he's a detective," Kathleen said. "Does he normally keep you guys in the loop 24/7? He questioned all of us regarding the strange old lady."

Willard scratched his head. "Actually, lately he's been less and less forthcoming with the details of his investigations. Tell you what. Why don't we do some driving around, maybe some of your extrasensory powers will tell us where he is? I wanted to comb an area along Highway 17 anyway."

"Okay." She had to start somewhere.

A few minutes later they sat in Willard's marked police car. He pulled out a Colts Mild cigar, glanced at her questioningly. "Do you mind?"

"It's your car," Kathleen said and they pulled away.

He asked her questions about her paranormal investigations as they drove, claiming local townsfolk viewed her as a hero—a possessed woman who helped save lives, bringing down a powerful evil force. Kathleen nodded and said yes and no at the appropriate times. She tried to keep her answers short, wanting to focus her energy on what her mind was telling her regarding Redmond's disappearance.

It seemed that Willard got the hint because a few minutes later he fell silent and let her dictate where they searched. They headed east out of town, along scenic Highway 17, took a few side roads that led to the ocean, stopped briefly at a few spots and carried on. Kathleen only shook her head each time they stopped, telling Willard she didn't feel anything, other than she was sure the house where Redmond was being held captive "fronted the ocean."

"Let's check Panmure beach," she said as they pulled back on the highway from Old Wharf Road. A dark feeling had suddenly enveloped her mind and she wanted to visit the scenic beach.

Concern etched Willard's brow as he noticed Kathleen's features darken. "Is the house there?"

"I don't know. But something's there."

The clouds had just started to roll out to sea as they pulled into the parking lot of Panmure beach, but the wind had intensified, the ocean waves growing, splashing up on the faded red sand. The late afternoon sun was starting to make its descent. Kathleen noticed six cars in the parking lot as Willard parked and shut off the ignition.

They parked beside a young couple necking in a newer orange Volkswagon Beetle and a blonde woman withdrew her lips from her surprised male companion and fumbled with her bathing suit, pulling it up over a large pair of breasts seconds after Willard was treated to a bird's eye view. He smiled and waved his index finger jokingly.

Kathleen looked over, raising an eyebrow.

"Hey, that wasn't my fault. I'm a healthy red-blooded Canadian," Willard said. "And a bachelor to boot."

The woman's face flushed red, her male companion started the Beetle and they exited just as Kathleen and Willard exited the cop car.

"Get a room," the cop said as they pulled out of the parking lot. "There are better places to do that."

They walked down the path through the bushes to the beach. There wasn't much unusual going on. One family with two small kids sat in lawn chairs under an umbrella, chatting and watching their kids play in the sand. Two teenagers threw a Frisbee. Two couples sat in the sand, noticed the cop, and tried to conceal a cooler of beer under a small towel. It was still illegal to drink beer on a public beach in PEI.

There were six others—three young men and three young women—playing beach volleyball.

"Let's take a walk," Willard said.

They walked along the beach, close to the water, Kathleen eyeing the people curiously. Nothing seemed out of the ordinary at first, but then she noticed an argument break out among the volleyball players. One of them had picked up a decorative wine bottle, started taking swigs, passing it around to his friends.

"Over there," she said to Willard, pointing to the group. They were about a hundred feet away. "That's going to get ugly."

Willard snapped off the leather clasp securing his handgun, picking up his pace and pulling out his radio. He wasn't leaving anything to chance. "Request back up, Panmure beach, immediately."

The voices had grown louder and angrier. By the time they were within fifty feet, all the players were enraged and yelling at one another. Suddenly one of the boys attacked another one, pushing him to the sand violently, jumping on top of him, clawing at his eyes. The smaller boy on the bottom screamed as blood gushed from his eyes.

"Get off him," Willard ordered. His walk had transformed into a full-tilt sprint toward the fighters.

But the calls were ignored. The larger boy gouged out an eye, waved it around in the air, put it in his mouth and chomped on it while his victim screamed and contorted in pain.

Meanwhile, all the others were fighting. Two of the women rolled around the sand, pulling large tufts of hair from each other's heads, scratching at faces, tearing the tiny bikini tops off.

Willard dove on the attacker who had just eaten the eyeball, knocking him off the screaming victim, pinning him to the ground.

Two other males were engaged in a heated boxing match. Both of their faces were cut and swollen as they stood toe-to-toe and traded blows, smiling and bleeding.

Kathleen approached one of the females, who had her victim pinned to the sand and was gouging large chunks of flesh out of her face with her long nails, grabbed her by the hair and yanked her off the screaming and bleeding victim.

Before she could get up, Kathleen delivered a well-placed kick to her jaw, watching two teeth become airborne, instantly knocking her unconscious.

Other people on the beach gawked in horror.

The bleeding victim rose, eyed Kathleen maliciously, and slowly walked toward her. Blood covered her face and impaired her vision as she flailed her arms six or seven feet from where Kathleen stood.

Kathleen sidestepped her and ran toward Willard, who was now being attacked from behind by the one-eyed man he had just saved. It's a good thing she had started working out lately. She delivered a well-aimed flying knee to the side of the man's face, knocking him out cold.

The blood-soaked woman stumbled toward the two boxers, who had decided, at least for the moment, to start taking pot-shots at her. Hearing police sirens, Kathleen turned toward the three and advanced as they delivered shockingly hard blows to the woman's face.

She had to think twice before getting in the middle of that melee, watching the bloodied woman absorb at least six hard shots to the face before her knees buckled and she dropped to the sand.

It didn't take long for the police and ambulance drivers to arrive. Six cops cuffed and stuffed the violent offenders into cop cars and ambulances. By that time, their rage had dissipated. They looked wide-eyed, wondering what in the hell had come over them so suddenly.

About an hour later, after some questioning had been completed, the tainted bottle safely in an evidence bag and on route to the lab for analysis, Kathleen and Willard sat on the sand close the water's edge. Everyone had left, but for the couple far away who had resumed sitting under the umbrella and watching their kids play in the sand. They weren't going to let a violent, rage-filled, gory battle spoil an otherwise pleasant day in paradise.

Willard sported a cut above his left eye and a black eye which paramedics had attended to.

Luckily, Kathleen was none the worse for wear—at least physically.

"Thanks," Willard said, sliding out a cigar, peeling the plastic wrap off, lighting it and taking a long drag. "That was some pretty good stuff. You saved my life."

"Don't mention it," Kathleen said, staring out at the ocean. The clouds had disappeared, the ocean waters now calm and tranquil, the late afternoon sun warming her darkened spirits. Gentle waves lapped at the shore. *What the fuck just happened?*

"Is it safe to say you owe me one?" she asked after a few minutes of silence.

"I owe you one."

Chapter Fourteen

"I owe you one," Beatrice Maling announced to Detective Redmond early that evening as she took the branding iron she had been heating with a propane torch and pushed the fiery orange luminescent and inverted pentagram hard onto his chest.

It hissed as it burned, spirals of smoke slowly drifting into the air. Beatrice inhaled deeply and grinned. She loved the sweet smell of burning flesh in the evening.

The detective howled in pain, writhing, hopelessly tugging at the ropes binding his wrists.

She removed the iron, placed it in a bucket of cold water that sizzled and bubbled over as it cooled the hot metal. "There. Now you have one of our symbols. This one even has the satanic goat in the middle of it, so there's no mistaking it."

The detective's face was still knotted as he glanced down at the blistering and bloody mark on the left side of his chest. *How am I going to get out of here?*

As she returned to her table of black magic accoutrements, he gathered his thoughts and tried to formulate some kind of a logical plan. One that would end the slow torture he had suffered since his captivity a few days ago. How many days now? He didn't remember anymore, as he was in perpetual darkness, occasionally blindfolded, prodded and poked and bombarded with eerie music from a small ghetto blaster hanging on a wire beside the only incandescent light bulb in a corner.

It seemed this evil woman was intent on driving him mad.

He drank at least one of her potions which had permeated his mind with dark thoughts; images of fiery devils, people screaming in torture, impossible sexual positions, gruesome deaths, all of it and then some had flooded his mind, most of it to blaring music.

The potion had eventually rendered him unconscious. Again, for how long, he had no idea. The only nourishment he had been allowed was gulps of water from a bucket and when Beatrice held it to his mouth, she poured quickly, spilling down his face and body, now mixing with the blood from his wounds. Beside the inverted pentagram, he had a knife slash on his chest, a line of blood mixed with water snaking down, across his white underwear, down his leg and along his foot, now forming a small pool of sticky blood below his toes that added to his discomfort.

She had also sliced four small incision-like cuts; two across the tops of his forearms and two along the calves of his legs. Those cuts also marked trails of blood that flowed to the cold dirt floor below.

Maybe she was planning to bleed him out to a slow death. He didn't know, but he had been unable to get much information from her other than "very soon you will have some company."

And of course he knew the reason for her attack. She wanted revenge, plain and simple, for the destruction of the spirit of James Maling, which he, along with specific members of PEIPI, had orchestrated.

He had only one chance, and he didn't know if it would work. The mentally challenged and deformed ape of a man that Beatrice had recruited, Bob, had entered the cellar on a few occasions, performing various tasks for his domineering master. Redmond had tried to befriend Bob on all but one occasion—when he was under a nasty bout of hallucinations from the potion—and it seemed he had been making some headway.

Bob was starting to smile at him.

He was trying to get the ape close to him, so he could remove the knife he carried in the top pocket of his greasy coveralls, cut the ropes binding him and escape hell on Earth. He might even decide to kill the two, or at least Beatrice. Bob was likely just a manipulated pawn in her master plan, whatever that might be. Bob couldn't help it. He was born mentally deficient, or had ended up that way as the result of some nasty head trauma, or maybe even an evil potion. It didn't matter either way to Redmond. He just thought if he could spare anyone's life, it would be the ape. Unless he got violent, of course. Then he wouldn't hesitate to plunge the knife right through his heart. But first he had to get it.

Beatrice was making him really angry. And Redmond, when he had his wits about him, wasn't the kind of guy you wanted to piss off. He had a bad temper that over the years he had struggled hard to control, even attending anger management courses in his early twenties after bashing in the heads of a few bullies so violently they had ended up in the hospital, one almost dying from his injuries. His face had been so badly beaten, he was barely recognizable.

And he didn't feel any remorse to this day. He absolutely despised bullies and felt they got what was coming to them. If the opportunity presented itself, he would do it all over again—of course now within the confines of the law.

If he felt remorse about anything, it was about the lack of attention he had devoted to his loyal wife, Jeanette, lately. Sure, they had had their ups and down, she wanted kids and he had talked her out of it, but she was a devoted and loyal woman who had taken great pains to ensure his happiness. There for him when he needed her, always ready to talk and comfort him when he got down over difficult cases, a great lover, a tender smile, a respectful, attractive and devoted woman. He could have done a lot worse. But lately, he had not been appreciating her at all, had crawled inside a shell, the horrific events of the past overshadowing and blocking the path to a healthy relationship.

What did it all mean, really, his preoccupation with the past? He couldn't change any of it now so what was the point in stewing over it? Sure, there was a grieving period that he would naturally be going through as a result of losing his friends in the fire, in the murders. But didn't the town view him as a hero for his role in ridding the town of the evil that could have festered out of control, infected the whole island population, spread like a plague through the entire country? Sure, he wanted to solve it with far less deaths. But, you can't please everyone all the time. Right?

Right.

He decided in that moment, in the context of his current dilemma, tied up and dying—he was slowly bleeding to death—the thing that mattered the most right now was to make Jeanette happy, be there for her instead of wallowing in self-pity. And he vowed to himself, if he could only get out of here alive, he would change the course of his life, concentrate more on the things that really mattered—like cultivating what once was a healthy relationship. Sad but true, when you realize your life could be snatched away from you at any second, it's also when you start to wonder if you have lived your life without any regrets.

And the answer that came to Redmond was a resounding no.

Beatrice, mixing up another potion, had suddenly stopped. She held up a vial and, realizing it was empty, grimaced, the network of wrinkles lining her face darkening. She clicked off the ghetto blaster. "Bob ... Bob ... bring some chicken blood down here will you?"

Silence.

Louder, "Bob ... Bob ... would you get down here with some chicken blood you imbecile?"

Silence.

Grinning, she turned to Redmond, her face barely visible in the darkness. "You stay right here, young man. You just can't get good help these days." And she left.

I owe you one, you fucking witch.

A few minutes later, Bob lumbered down the stairs, a metal bucket in tow. Redmond had managed to loosen the rope binding his right hand. "Bob, how are you my friend? Long time no see. What you up to?"

Bob, his matted brown hair jutting off at odd angles, acknowledged the detective with a childish grin and set the bucket on the table. He had a tumor the size of a grapefruit protruding from his right temple and resembled an overgrown troll. His eyes, deeply set in his Frankenstein skull, were barely visible.

Bob turned and grunted. Then he opened his mouth, like he was trying to say something, suddenly cast his gaze to the ground, and closed it again.

"Help me, Bob. I'm thirsty." Waving his right finger, pointing to the water bucket. "Bring the water, please. I'm dying of thirst." Truth be told, the detective was dying of thirst, his throat dry and parched.

Moreover, he was dying from the slow but steady loss of blood.

Bob looked around the room and his gaze stopped at the stairs leading to the exit. He frowned.

"She's not here, Bob. She's not coming back right away. The water ... please ... please!"

Bob hesitated, looked furtively at the stairway again, then scooped up the water bucket and carried it over to the detective.

"That's it," Redmond said. As Bob neared, Redmond took advantage of the moment, pulling his loose hand free, snatching the knife from Bob's top pocket and waving it threateningly. "I don't want to hurt you. Just back away."

Bob took a few steps back. This time he did speak in a slow and mentally challenged way: "Beatrice ... Beatrice ... she won't like."

"Fuck Beatrice and the broom she rode in on," Redmond said, cutting his arms, then his legs free. Bob's ugly face contorted into what at first appeared to be rage, but then the detective realized it was something else. This man was afraid of him.

And he was well-trained in supervising a situation where he held the upper hand. "Just back away, Bob. I won't hurt you if you back away ... stay put. I'm going to get you out of here."

Bob cowered in the corner while the detective grabbed a small flashlight from the table, flashed the beam around the floor and located a pile of clothes—his and some others. How many people had this demented woman tortured and killed? He quickly dressed and was about to leave, when he noticed a samurai sword next to a stuffed doll collection. The dolls eerily resembled PEIPI members.

He hurriedly grabbed the dolls, stuffing them in his pockets, picked up the sword, felt the blade for sharpness—razor sharp—and scanned Bob, whose face had brightened, perhaps sensing he may also have a chance at freedom.

Redmond had no idea what sort of trauma Bob had suffered, but he imagined it was very likely much worse than the hardships and horror he had witnessed as a police detective. "You're coming with me, right?"

Bob nodded eagerly. His mannerisms were like a little kid.

Flashlight in one hand and samurai sword in the other, Redmond stealthily crept up the stairs. Bob waited until he was halfway up and then followed. Redmond felt weak and dizzy as he breathed in the cool night air, stepping outside on the overgrown lawn. He quickly appraised his whereabouts in the faint light of the moon. The house was in the middle of a one-acre clearing with a barn and a couple of smaller outbuildings. The rest of the property was bordered by thick forest, but he saw what looked like a small clearing in the distance, *perhaps a path leading out of here. Didn't I hear a dog?*

He suddenly heard the shuffling of paws—running paws—charging from behind. He spun around and saw a pit bull rapidly closing the distance. This animal wasn't even barking. It was attacking in stealth mode. As it leaped into the air, Redmond swung the sword quickly, decapitating the dog.

The dog yelped—a short high-pitched squeal—its head flew into the air and its headless body ran about twenty feet from inertia before the legs buckled and it skidded along the grass to a stop, spewing blood like a water fountain.

Bob stood beside the detective watching, unmoving. He slowly smiled. There was no love lost between him and the pit bull.

"Let's go," Redmond said, waving him toward the forest. Redmond tried to run, but his weak legs weren't interested in obeying brain commands and he stumbled and fell, too weak from blood loss.

Bob grabbed him by the arm and jerked him to his feet. He was surprised at the man's strength.

"Focus, focus," he said to himself as Bob released his arm. He took one step, waited for the adrenaline to kick in. He heard the front door creak open and then felt it, fresh adrenaline, a built in turbo-charger exploding, pushing him forward. He ran for the cover of the trees, Bob following.

Perhaps twenty yards later, he heard it.

Click, click.

And there was no mistaking the sound. Beatrice had loaded a couple of cartridges into a gun, probably a shotgun. If there was one thing Redmond knew well, it was the sound different guns made as they were loaded.

Beatrice didn't even give them a warning. "Try and get away from me, will you?"

As he reached the small path leading into the forest, he turned, just in time to see something that surprised him and would disturb him for the rest of his life. Bob had stopped and turned around, facing Beatrice, arms outstretched, shielding the detective with his massive body.

"I want it," he said. The words leaving his lips sounded more like "I won it."

Beatrice stepped off the porch, leveled the gun and blew Bob's brains out. For an old bat, she was a pretty good shot. The detective saw Bob drop to the ground with a thud and roll, landing on his back, his arms outstretched, staring at the stars. In the days to come, what would help him deal with the gruesome image of Bob Bladen, lying on his back, his head blown open, grey matter and blood oozing out, a red pool of blood fanning out around his head, was the dead man's expression.

He was grinning, happy that in death he had finally found peace. Finally, found an escape from the torment that had been his life. Finally, was free from the clutches of his murderous captor. Finally, would no longer have to be an unwilling participant in the gruesome murders perpetrated by Beatrice Maling, would no longer have to participate in the macabre swath of carnage she was currently planning.

In death, Bob had found the tranquility that had evaded him in life. He willingly breathed his last breath and died.

But Redmond certainly wasn't going to hang around and orate a eulogy for this man he hardly knew but who had probably saved his life.

As he sprinted the last twenty feet to the forest, the shotgun blasted again and buckshot zinged past his head, wounded tree branches cracking, snapping and breaking off all around him.

He had only one thing on his mind right now. It wasn't revenge. He didn't have the strength for that anymore. That would have to wait. He wanted to get as far away as he could from the lair of this witch. And he wanted more than ever before to live.

Chapter Fifteen

"Live, love, and drink," Jacob said.

"You're drunk," Angela replied.

"I'm drunk, but I'm happy."

"Better that than drunk and sad," she said, reading a copy of *The Guardian* that Sunday afternoon as they sat in lawn chairs in their backyard, enjoying the hot afternoon sun, Angela sipping a glass of red wine while Jacob swilled his beer back.

Arriving home after the double paranormal investigations late Friday night, Jacob had informed Angela that the spirit of her abusive great-uncle Raymond Dodson had been released into hades. He would no longer be assaulting anyone. He could still remember the relieved expression on her face as she had heard the news, like a great anchor had been lifted from her mind and body. Her first reaction had been one of elation and then her brow slowly began to furrow as the scars she had tried to keep buried for so many years slowly resurfaced, serving as a bitter reminder of the hell and torture she had endured at his perverted hands.

Unable to contain the surge of emotions, she had put her hands to her face and began sobbing, the cries beginning as soft whimpers and then escalating into loud wracking sobs that reverberated through their conjugal home.

Jacob had stayed quiet the entire time, feeling it was better to let her deal with it in her own way, on her own time. Not to judge, but to comfort and listen, be there for her. Let her release it. So he had hugged Angela tightly and allowed her to vent the pain and hurtful memories. She had cried for perhaps fifteen minutes until finally she had no more tears left to cry with. She was all cried out.

After returning from the bathroom where she had cleaned herself up, splashing warm water on her tear-soaked face, he had noticed a more positive change in her demeanor. She had run downstairs quickly, returning with a bottle of red wine to celebrate, threw him a seductive smile, a look he hadn't seen in a very long time, and began to slowly peel her clothes off. It was late and Jacob was physically and mentally drained—but it had been long time since he had made love and his carnal desires superseded any urge he might have had to sleep. The little head was more than happy to do the thinking. Besides, he hadn't seen his girlfriend this happy in a long time.

Even though she was riding the swinging emotional pendulum, had gone from an extreme low and was now soaring to an extreme high, he wanted more than ever to join her on the upswing, jump on, thrust together in a passionate union of blissful ecstasy and mutually intense climactic fulfillment.

And that's exactly what they had done.

So, for the last two days, although Kathleen had briefed him on the violent brawl at Panmure beach yesterday, Jacob couldn't get the naked and thrusting image of Angela out of his mind. It had been the best sex he had ever had in his life and he didn't imagine the pleasing memory would ever disappear.

And the amazing sex had gone a hell of a long way to removing the black cloud from his mind. It was now a much weaker force, still there, but shrinking deep within the recesses of his mind. The joyful session had given him renewed faith in life, in his relationship—in his ability to one day rid himself completely of the black cloud's debilitating influence.

He smiled as the image of Angela's delectable naked body again flashed in his mind. *That's just how a man's mind works. Once he's had great sex, he can't stop thinking about it. And he wants it over and over and over again.*

As Angela busied herself reading the paper, he walked into the garage. A minute later he returned with a Colt's Mild. He had had a phone conversation with Mark recently, and Mark had filled him in on his bender with alcohol and the tiny cigars. He had said they "went a long way to relieve some of my stress."

And if Jacob had to be completely honest, he was troubled by the escalating levels of violence in and around this small town. And he had also noticed a fatigue—slowly occurring over the last three days—draining his energy level, making him perpetually tired. He had reasoned it was the result of his sexual tension, his battle with the black cloud, and creative burn-out. He had thrown himself into his work lately, churning out websites and copy at a brutal and astonishing pace. He had read that writers suffered from it as well, researched the symptoms on the internet, and they had matched up with his almost identically. They may as well have had his mug posted beside the article. *This is an example of the physical manifestation of burn-out. Note the bloodshot eyes, the dark circles under them, the agitation in this man's expression.*

Everything had caught up to him. He had hit the wall, crashed and burned.

His body and mind were now in recovery mode. To heal properly, he would need a few stress-free days away from work, relaxing and doing the things that brought him joy.

But, after the amazing night with Angela, he had pushed it all away, believing then it would go away, bought a pack of

Colts and snuck a few puffs yesterday and earlier today, not wanting Angela to notice that he had taken up a new hobby.

What the hell, he thought through the buzz beginning to envelop and comfort his mind. *My relationship is back on track and we'll fix whatever fucked-up problem that comes up. We always do. Take a few days off work. Have a few drinks. Be right as rain soon enough.*

So, although he probably should have listened to the demands of his body telling him to go to sleep, get caught up, he pushed the mental and physical fatigue out of his mind, peeled the plastic off the tiny cigar and smoked. He had quit five years ago, but was now slowly developing a psychological and physical addiction that he was not prepared to admit to.

Life is good. Enjoy the time with Angela. Rebuild the fire. You know how much she turns you on.

"What're you doing?" Angela said, looking up from her paper.

"I'm just having a little cigar to celebrate our new lease on life."

Angela was about to protest but thought better of it. Although she wasn't a big fan of smoking, she remembered grimly where her protests had gotten with respect to her ex-husband, Aaron and his cigarette addiction. In no uncertain terms, he had said, "Why don't you shut the fuck up and mind your own fucking business." *Pick your battles,* she thought. Besides, she knew Jacob had been fighting some inner demons of his own lately and if he needed to blow off some steam right now so be it. Who knew what kind of horrific events he had just witnessed contending with that sexual pervert what's-his-name the other day.

"Don't make a habit of it," she said, pointing to her empty wine glass. "Would you mind?"

"Not at all, my dear." He took the wine glass, kissed her on the cheek with a loud puckering sound, and went inside the house.

Meanwhile, Angela's face darkened, reading an article in *The Guardian*.

Violent Brawl Erupts At Panmure Beach

An otherwise peaceful and sunny day turned ugly and violent Saturday afternoon as six people playing beach volleyball suddenly and inexplicably became enraged and started beating on each other, resulting in the death of one woman.

Maureen Magnussen, 25, was pronounced dead from severe head trauma a few minutes after arriving at King's County Memorial Hospital, according to Police Constable Russ Willard, who was at the beach when the violence erupted and sustained a black eye and cut above his head trying to contain it.

"I was walking on the beach, when all of a sudden these people became agitated, started beating on each other," he said. "And they wouldn't stop. So, in the interests of trying to save some lives, I got involved."

According to Willard, local paranormal talent Kathleen Freeborne was also at the scene and jumped into the fray.

"She saved my life," he said.

Freeborne declined comment, other than to say she does not view herself as a hero.

Police are still investigating the cause of the sudden violence and trying to determine what charges will be laid and to whom, according to Willard. He refused to speculate if the incident is connected in any way to the mysterious disappearance of Detective Blaine Redmond, who was investigating a sudden rage incident involving Mark Riley when the detective vanished last week. He is still missing.

"Since it's an ongoing investigation, I can't comment on what, if any, clues we have," Willard said.

Peter Givens, whose eye was gouged from its socket in the melee, remains in hospital in good condition. Joanne and Dean Wilson, Daryl Hansen and Bridget Philips were treated for their injuries and released.

"What do you want to do today?" Jacob asked, returning with the drinks and plucking his smoking cigar from the ashtray. "Want to go to the beach?"

"I'm not so sure about that," Angela said. Her soft features had become pale. "Have you read this?" she asked, handing him the paper as he reclined in a soft bed-style lawn chair.

Jacob grimaced as he scanned the article. "Kathleen told me about it, but I didn't know someone had died."

"What do you think about it?"

"It's terrible."

"Do you have any theories?"

"Yeah, I think Redmond's disappearance is connected to this. It has to do with the old lady, which none of us got a good description of, and that moonshine Mark was drinking. That shit's poison rage."

"Shouldn't we be doing something about it? Instead of sitting around here partying?"

"I don't know." But, the more Jacob thought about it, the more it did start to bother him. Hadn't he and detective Redmond become decent, if not good friends? Hadn't the detective saved his life during the heated battle with the evil spirit of James Maling? Yes, he had.

And, wasn't he now in the detective's debt for taking a bullet for him? Yes, he was. Scratching his two-day growth, inhaling deeply on the cigar, he decided something should be done. Angela was right once again. He had been so absorbed with his own problems—he now felt ashamed of it—he hadn't given the detective much thought.

"Let's call Kathleen," Angela said finally. "She always knows what to do."

Jacob was about to call her when his phone rang. It was Kathleen. *Great minds think alike,* Jacob thought, grinning. He wasn't prepared to entertain the flip side.

"Are you guys up for another paranormal investigation tonight?" Kathleen asked after they had dispensed with the small talk.

He had her on speaker phone. "Do you think this has anything to do with Redmond's disappearance?"

"I think it has everything to do with it."

Chapter Sixteen

"Do you want to do everything?" Kathleen asked Mark as he packed the recording gear into Black Death later that evening in preparation for their trip over to Eva Santire's house, a few miles north of the town of Souris.

As Eva had talked to Kathleen a few hours earlier, Mark's face had turned an ashen-white watching her. And, before she had even hung up the phone, he was already curbside loading duffle bags of equipment into Black Death.

Something was wrong. How did he know a call would come in that day, the team would agree to an investigation, and they would head out that night? After she had hung up she had asked Mark about it and he just shook his head and said he had some "feeling" about it but couldn't nail down the source of the feeling. Explaining it to her, there had been confusion etched in his brow, as if he was bewildered by the whole thing but somehow knew they would be going ... had to go really. But, she wasn't able to get anything more out of him, so she had attempted to help him with the gear.

That's when he had stopped her and said: "No, it's okay, you've been through a lot lately, you need your energy. Please let me do it." Finally, after watching him come and go, now on the third trip, Kathleen had grown impatient and wanted to help.

He looked at her blankly, a tripod in hand. "It's done. There's nothing else left but to wait for Angela and Jacob. Did you say they were coming?"

"Mark, I told you that twice already. What's wrong with you?"

"Look," he said suddenly. A moment of clarity. "Are you sure you want to do this? Why don't you just let the rest of us handle it? We can do it on our own you know."

"Mark, I'm the one that has the sixth sense here," Kathleen said, finally willing to admit to her extrasensory perception. She may as well come to terms with it. The whole town talked about it. And, who knew, if things went to shit in a handbasket at work, maybe she could actually hang a shingle up and capitalize on all this popularity. Might be worth a shot. Things hadn't been going particularly well at work lately anyway. And things with Baglund were bound to come to a head eventually. She was that close to telling him to fuck right off!

Sometimes a change was as good as a vacation. No point in hiding behind this power and pretending it wasn't there when she could develop it, maybe use it to improve people's lives, solve their problems?

"Kathleen I do not have a good feeling about this one. One part of me wants to tell you to come, but there's another side saying quite the opposite. Stay home, please!"

"Why are you so insistent?"

"I don't know. Something about the kidnapping. I'm getting dark flashes, little tidbits of memory that won't quite form. But the memories are all dark, all dangerous. And, somehow I feel I'm in danger and you're in danger just by me telling you this."

Kathleen could now feel the panic starting to rear its ugly head. Good thing she had popped two panic pills a couple of hours ago, the drowsiness they created only now beginning to dull her senses, gap her out for periods. She took a few deep breaths and tried the metaphor trick her counselor had instructed her during a recent phone conversation.

I'm a flowing river, moving easily and effortlessly downstream, my problems dissipating, disappearing with every white water wave that crashes up on shore as the water crests the big boulders, finally floating out into a wide open and still lake. The water is so calm it's like glass. I am the calm water, looking up into the sky, the small clouds, the sun, the mountains. The water is me and I am the water. The water is calm and still. I am calm and still.

She had gapped out during the exercise, had unintentionally closed her eyes in an effort to induce a meditative trance, one that would leave her with a sense of inner peace and the courage and calmness she would need for the danger that certainly lurked ahead.

Mark was staring at her when she opened her eyes. "Besides," she said, picking up where she had left off, "what if Liz wants to help with this haunting?" She was about to swear but the metaphoric exercise had, at least for the time being, stripped her of the need to use profanity to make her point. "Who the heck do you think she will channel through?"

Mark knew it was a rhetorical question, so he only nodded.

"And I'm worried about Redmond. I think the only way for us to find him is through the door of that house," Kathleen said.

There was a honk outside. Angela and Jacob had arrived. It was time to leave.

A few minutes later they rolled northeast down Highway 4, the easy friendship they had once shared no longer visible in the rumbling cab of Black Death. Angela, Jacob, and Mark sat silently while Kathleen brought them up to speed. Eva Santire, a widow in her mid-forties, had experienced a rash of nasty attacks lately, some of them so violent she had the physical scars to prove it. Her old house, to listen to her version of events, had at one time been used for black magic by a coven of witches sometime around the late 1800's.

Apparently during a witch hunt, about six of them who had practiced their craft together in the house they shared, had been rounded up and burned alive at a huge bonfire in the town square of Souris to the joyous and celebrative cheers of local townsfolk. Well, as it turned out the coven had returned with a vengeance to the old home secluded on ten acres. They were bent on driving Eva out of the house she had purchased, with the intention of renovating, three years ago. They had driven out all the contractors through a series of accidents.

The exterior painter had his scaffolding collapse. He came crashing down and suffered a broken leg. Another carpenter's nail gun had apparently turned on him, shooting him twice in the shoulder, three times in the arm before he had high-tailed it out of there, not even bothering to try and return for his tools. And two painters who had worked together for a decade with little drama had suddenly turned on each other and ended up in a violent fistfight that had left them both bloodied and battered with no interest in returning to the property. Again, they decided it was not in their best interest to return for their rollers and paint brushes.

Eva had had both arms mysteriously pierced with sharp objects but had no idea where they had come from. She had been gardening when she was suddenly and mysteriously speared. As well, her ankle had been severely burned, she had several gashes on her legs and just recently she had stepped on a wasp's nest and suffered multiple stings. She swore the wasp's nest had mysteriously appeared.

When Kathleen had asked her why she didn't just leave, her answer had been plain and simple; "I have no family, very little money, and no place else to go."

Kathleen hadn't bothered to delve into her financial or family situation. She wasn't a counselor, she was a ghost hunter. Let someone else have that job. She had enough on her plate.

They were about ten minutes away from the property, by the time Kathleen had finished the briefing. "You guys have any questions? Angela, are you sure you're up for this?"

The diminutive woman didn't look very confident. "All I know is if I didn't come along and something happened to one of you guys, something that I could have prevented, I wouldn't be able to live with myself."

Kathleen looked at Jacob. "And you?" He looked a little more refreshed than he had earlier. After the news about the paranormal investigation, the voice of reason had prevailed and he had crawled into bed with Angela and they had slept soundly for about four hours before they had awoken to get ready for tonight. He still felt a little groggy, but had slept off the four or five beers, eaten a hearty steak dinner with Angela, and was as prepared as he would ever be.

"I'm good to go," he said.

"Mark?"

There was a pause. He seemed mesmerized by the road in front of him, lulled into a daydream state by the rumble of Black Death.

"Mark, you okay?"

"You want the truth or you want a lie."

"The truth. Always the truth."

"I'm scared shitless. As I said I don't have a good feeling about this. And I'm not the psychic one here."

"But, you're good to go?" Kathleen asked. "Because if you want to back out, now's the time to do it. I wouldn't blame you if you did."

"You heard what Angela said?"

"Yeah."

"Well that's my sentiment as well."

Kathleen only nodded. What else was she going to say? She was now the official medium, the one in charge of this operation, and she had slowly but steadily felt her heart rate increase, her palms become sweatier, the closer Black Death got to the house of horror. She was no longer the dead calm lake. She felt more like a thundering waterfall of emotion. They were all in the same boat, directly in the destructive path of a tsunami wave, threatening to rain down its deadly and devastating force into their already unsteady existence.

"Wait a minute," Kathleen said. "What the hell was I thinking?"

"What?" Jacob asked, waiting for the big revelation. "What are you talking about?"

"Russ Willard. The cop. He owes me one." She pulled out her phone, speed-dialing the constable. "We need you for back-up," she said after a while. After a short conversation, she hung up the phone and smiled, not her most cheerful smile—far from it—but the best one she had in her repertoire at the moment. It would have to do. "He's going to be around, in case we need him."

Angela and Jacob uttered a collective sigh, while Mark kept steady to the wheel. They had arrived. He pulled into the winding driveway that eventually led to a mammoth two-story Victorian style house, one that in its glory days had clearly been built for a local dignitary, or at the very least upper-crust aristocracy. It had splendid architecture, overhangs, decorative woodwork, and massive wraparound deck that in better days would have been a sitting area reserved for gentry.

But its glory had long faded. The grey paint was peeling from the wooden siding, the shingles were curling, and bits and pieces of the decorative woodwork were falling off, some clinging stubbornly to a bygone age of splendor and grandeur.

Broken scaffolding lay strewn on the overgrown grass in front, assorted paint cans and rollers scattered about, a grim testament to the evil force shrouding the forbidding, dilapidated home. Thick vines had overgrown much of the exterior, covering at least three windows.

Dead trees with broken branches dotted the property, still standing as if waiting for a rebirth. Stripped of their greenery, they were but a shadow of their former selves.

Kathleen felt it immediately after Black Death had turned into the driveway. A dark and evil force so powerful it had chilled her blood, made the hairs on the back of her neck stand up so rigid she thought they would pierce through her blue cotton shirt. It was like a black cloud hung over the acreage. She felt like screaming, turning the vehicle around, getting as far away from this dark spectacle ASAP, even though she despised the acronym.

But Willard had been quick to point out they had not made any headway in the hunt for Redmond. And she felt the only way to him was through the front door of this decrepit building. What choice did she have? This was her fate, her destiny, depending on how events transpired.

Mark killed the ignition and the team was silent for a few seconds. Suddenly he leaned over and kissed Kathleen passionately on the lips. "I love you so much."

"I love you too, Mark," she said, surprised at the sudden outflow of emotion.

Angela took her cue. "I know I haven't been the best girlfriend lately, and I'm so sorry. I love you, Jacob, more than you know." She leaned over and kissed him long and full on the mouth.

"I love you too, sweetie," he said when she finally released him from the embrace. "Don't worry, you've had a lot of shit to deal with."

Kathleen stepped out of the truck, took a deep breath, and walked up the overgrown path to the entrance. The others grabbed a few bags and followed.

They were greeted—if you could call it that—at the front door by a somber and petrified woman with wavy red hair, blue jeans, and a white t-shirt. The middle-aged woman was covered in bandages. Both arms were wrapped in gauze and cotton baton, her left arm was in a makeshift sling made from a torn bed sheet and small skin-colored bandages dotted her otherwise pretty face and neck, evidently the result of the recent wasp attack. Her blue eyes were wide with shock and she had dark circles and wrinkles forming around them. She looked like she hadn't gotten a good night's sleep in a long time. The left cuff of her jeans was rolled up, the lower leg bandaged with gauze.

She had a slender but muscular frame and if hadn't been for the horrific accidents of late, she would probably be spending her evening jogging or lifting weights at the gym. In spite of the petrified demeanor, she definitely had the appearance that she could handle herself in a brawl. It was in the eyes—street-smarts and savvy that belied her panicked exterior.

"I'm Eva," she said. "Thanks for coming."

Everyone was introduced and they walked into the living room. The place was a construction zone, with tools still scattered haphazardly, dust coating the covered furniture, and boards with nails poking up dangerously, still littering the floor. But the rooms were spacious, the floor plan good. The home might have had potential as a fixer-upper if it weren't for the witches, who had their own agenda with respect to the property, their home at one time.

Kathleen felt the dark energy in the home, much more intense than outside in the moonlit darkness. It permeated every fiber of her being and made it difficult to concentrate. She brushed the sweat off her brow in the kitchen as Eva brought them up to speed on current events. She said she had recently heard knocking sounds coming from the master bedroom upstairs and an eerie scraping sound from the undeveloped cellar. Her face was a pale white, her eyes anxious.

They agreed to split up, with Angela and Jacob covering the upstairs while Kathleen and Mark would inspect the basement. With flashlights in hand and Jacob carrying a small hammer, they crept up the creaky stairs while Angela and Mark disappeared downstairs. Eva agreed to stay in the kitchen, no longer wanting any part of the evil force at work in her home.

"Are you okay?" Jacob asked, glancing at Angela as she stopped in the middle of the stairs.

"I'm getting scared."

"Do you want to stay downstairs?"

She paused before deciding. "No."

"Okay, let's go."

When they arrived on the dimly lit landing, the full moon illuminating the upper hallway a blue-grey from a small window, they heard it. A rapping sound, coming from the master bedroom.

They froze, staring at each other with wide-eyed fear. Angela was trembling.

"If you're in there, please go away and quit tormenting the owner of this house," Jacob said. "Please stop."

Silence.

They slowly walked down the dark hall and entered the master bedroom, surveying the scene. Two large windows with sheer grey fabric coverings offered views to the treed property. But for a king-sized bed with crumpled blankets, two night tables with small antique bedside lamps, the room was sparsely furnished.

The sheers danced on the windows. The windows were closed.

Angela pointed to the fluttering movement with an unsteady hand.

Jacob looked and nodded. That's when it happened. And piecing together the memory some time later, Jacob would see it vividly etched in his mind but horrifically playing itself out in slow-motion, extending the maelstrom of intense emotion and sadness.

Angela was picked up, floated in the air momentarily, screaming, waving her hands, telling Jacob to "please do something."

He dropped the hammer, reached for her elevated leg, but she danced in the air higher, rising just beyond his reach. "Put her down, you motherfucker," he yelled.

And the evil force obeyed, slamming her into the wall violently. She withered down onto the floor, her legs splayed out at odd angles, her head tilted to the side, staring at Jacob, a pleading, panicked look in her eyes.

Jacob ran to her aid, but as he knelt down beside her he saw something that would haunt and torment him for the rest of his life. Blood suddenly sprayed out from a clean circular incision in Angela's heart, as if her body had been stabbed by an invisible sword.

Angela let out a short, shrill scream, her head lolled to one side and she died; mouth agape, eyes wide with fear and incomprehension.

"No, no, no," Jacob said, crying, while the blood squirted onto his face, chest, arms, and legs. Although he screamed loudly at the sight of his dead girlfriend, his mind did not register the panicked sounds. All was silent and dark inside a head swimming with emotion, overcome by an immense grief, sadness and sorrow at his loss. He was no longer within reach of his mental faculties as he hugged Angela tightly, the screams and sobs now distant and removed, seeming to echo from another body, another mind.

Kathleen and Mark rushed up the stairs to the sounds, stopped momentarily in the kitchen, where they gaped in horror at the body of Eva, impaled to the wall by a large sword that had been stabbed forcefully through her head. Her eyes were wide, her mouth open, a network of blood lines dripping down her forehead, into her eyes, covering her face and chest. And there was something else. The kitchen was on fire. Flames danced along the floor, quickly licking up the dated kitchen counter, rapidly devouring the cabinets.

They raced upstairs.

"Jacob, Jacob," Kathleen said, looking in shock at the dead body of her friend, gripping Jacob's shoulder. She stood behind him, Mark behind her. "We have to go. The house is on fire."

The fire was rapidly spreading through the main floor, the house filling with black smoke as the blaze crackled and popped, the heat becoming intense.

Kathleen opened her cell phone to call Willard while Mark tried to convince Jacob it was time to go. "Shit, no signal. What the hell's going on?"

The fire rapidly advanced down the hallway. Soon it would engulf the entire main floor and seal off the exit, trapping them in a fiery grave.

Mark tugged at Jacob, who clung to Angela. "Come on buddy. She would want you to live, help us end this thing."

"Leave me here," Jacob protested, the tears streaming down his bloodied face. "What do I have to live for now?"

"Revenge," Kathleen said. "Come on. Do it for Angela. We don't have much time."

Finally Mark and Kathleen were able to pry their friend loose from the corpse of Angela. He had insisted they bring her along, but glancing at the stairwell, now a forbidding wall of flame that was rapidly licking up the stairs, Kathleen turned to him and said: "If you want to live, Jacob, you'll have to leave her."

In the meantime, Mark had gathered three blankets from the bedrooms, was soaking them with water in the claw-foot tub in the bathroom.

He reappeared a little while later with three soaking wet blankets. "Come on you guys. We have to go. Now!!"

A voice of reason had suddenly calmed Jacob's tormented and grieving mind. He was motivated by the need for revenge, and he had vowed to exact it with a raging fury so fierce that the person responsible for this macabre spectacle would regret the day they had ever been born.

They wrapped themselves quickly in the blankets and Mark went first, slowly stepping down the stairs. Once he felt the intense heat of the fire, he ran through the wall of flame, burst through the door with a crash, landed on the porch, rolling, peeling the wet blanket off and standing up.

"You go," Kathleen said, pointing at the firewall. She was sure if she left Jacob he would change his mind, stay and burn to death.

He nodded, walked a few steps down the stairs, ran and burst through the firewall and out onto the porch. By the time he peeled off the wet blanket, his hair was ablaze, but Mark quickly picked up a wet blanket and smothered the flames before they could begin burning flesh.

Kathleen took a few steps and ran, feeling the heat singe her eyebrows as she burst through the fireball. Mark grabbed her before she could fall, patted down a small fire which had appeared on the back of her long brown hair.

They stood outside in the darkness and watched the house quickly turn into a huge fireball, the flames quickly devouring it.

Kathleen picked up her phone. Still no signal. Then she heard a metallic click and jerked her head around quickly.

"The heroes of the island," Beatrice Maling said, leveling a shotgun. "We finally meet in the flesh."

Chapter Seventeen

I would sure like to meet you under different circumstances, Kathleen thought, twisting and struggling hopelessly with the ropes binding her arms and legs. She had just woken up, blinking, adjusting to the dim light from the single bulb illuminating the dark cellar and noticed the legs of an old woman, Beatrice Maling, she now knew, making her way up the rickety stairs and out of the basement prison.

But for a black lace bra and panties, Kathleen was bound naked to the wall.

She glanced around the small room, slowly recognizing the other prisoners. Detective Redmond, tattered clothing, multiple cuts, tied to the wall, hands and legs spread-eagled, his head tilted to one side. *Is he dead?*

Mark and Jacob, similarly tied, had been stripped to their underwear. Their eyes were closed, heads tilted down. *Are they dead?*

How could we have been so stupid? How could I have been so stupid? In light of everything I've been through, leading the team to that insane, possessed property. It had been a trap, even Mark had suspected that. Why didn't I listen to him? At least bring the police along to the investigation. But no, I had to charge forward, like some invincible superhero and lead us into a trap. And lead Angela to her death. How can I live with myself now, after this? If I ever get out of this, I think I'm giving up this shit. It's too hard on me, too hard on Mark. Look at him, tied to a wall, incarcerated. Surely this witch, she told us her name before she injected us, Beatrice Maling, doesn't intend to let us walk away from this. What does she want? Hey, you're the still calm lake. Be the still calm lake and think yourself through this. Still, calm, clear waters. Lucid and thoughtful.

"Mark," Kathleen said. Nothing. "Mark, Mark, wake up."

Nothing.

"Jacob, Jacob, wake up."

Dead calm.

"Redmond, Redmond, wake up. Please Detective Redmond, wake up. We need you."

The detective's eyes slowly opened. He glanced around at his new neighbors, finally fixing his gaze on Kathleen. "You," he said in a weak voice. "You're here."

Some of his cuts had been bandaged with white gauze. Beatrice had decided to preserve his life for a little longer, after finally catching up with him along the trail leading to the ocean. She would at least allow him to die among friends—maybe even let him witness a few of their deaths before she killed him.

As long as he behaved himself.

In his haste to escape, he had tripped over an outstretched branch, fell and hit his head on a rock, knocking himself out. She had been elated to find him but disappointed that she had only recovered one Voodoo doll, the one resembling Angela. And last night, while talking to her unwilling guest, she had tossed the doll recklessly against the basement wall and then rammed a pin through its heart.

"I'm here," Redmond acknowledged wearily. "Where's Angela?" He knew but wanted confirmation.

Kathleen paused, her eyes welling with tears. "She didn't make it. Died in one of our investigations."

"I know."

"Any ideas?" she asked Redmond.

"No. I almost got away, but fell and knocked myself out. She shot her helper, Bob, before finally finding me unconscious in the woods."

Mark slowly came to, blinking and looking around in horror.

Jacob opened his eyes and registered the same reaction. "I feel dizzy. She must have drugged us."

"We have to get out of here," Kathleen said. "Blaine, you must have some ideas?"

"I tried. I almost made it too. But we have to be careful." He pointed to the table of Voodoo dolls. A charred Voodoo doll sat on the table, along with others in various stages of production. "We're dealing with an evil, modern-day witch here. That's how Angela was killed. And she used a Voodoo doll to torture me."

Jacob frowned.

They heard the basement door creak and swing open, basking the dimly lit dungeon in bright sunlight before the door slammed shut and the faint light prevailed. Beatrice Maling entered the prison. Absent were the cane and limp, one-time symbols of her handicap. She had fixed an elixir potion that for now had healed the ailing leg, given her a vitality and strength that belied her eighty-five years.

"How are my guests doing?" she said.

"Fuck you, bitch," Jacob said. "I hope you rot in hell."

"Oh, I've been to hell and back, young man," she said. "And believe me, it's not a place where people rot."

"Fuck you," Jacob said.

"You'd be wise to keep your mouth shut," she said, purposefully striding over to the table. She picked up the charred remains of the doll that once resembled Angela. "This is what remains of your girlfriend." And she tossed the doll hard into the wall, and it shattered into a million black pieces.

"Fu ..."

"Now, now," she said, picking up another partially constructed doll, waving it in front of his face. "This is your friend Kathleen."

There was a moment's silence as they began to recognize the full weight of the fate that awaited them.

Beatrice continued. "And unless you want her to end up like Angela, you're going to listen to my instructions. I'll be mixing up a potion, a mixture that will persuade you to travel to the two small wells on the north side of Montague. I want you to contaminate those wells with my moonshine. I call it Poison Rage. I believe Mark's had the pleasure of sampling it. Mark, what did you think?"

Mark glared daggers at his captor, a rage unprovoked by any potion, burning in his veins.

"No comment. No problem." She approached Jacob, got to within inches of his face, holding the doll up to his eyes. "You will obey me or I will slice this doll to shreds and you'll see your friend die gruesomely before your very eyes."

Jacob, on the verge of exploding, looked at Kathleen's pleading expression.

"Don't worry," he said. "We'll get out of this some other way." Even though he knew of no other way, knew the situation was hopeless. After a minute or so, he slowly nodded his head.

"Good," Beatrice said. "I'm glad we got that out of the way. I'm going to make this town pay for what they put James Maling through, the humiliation and the indignities they subjected him to, before the likes of you guys came along and terminated his plan for revenge. Well, guess what? I'm going to take over where he left off. They'll pay, and you'll pay." She spun around, her eyes flaring red while examining them.

This woman is stark raving man, Kathleen decided, as Beatrice bent over the table and began mixing a potion with some vials. A few minutes later, she held it up and began chanting: "I call to the power of Satan to help me in my quest to avenge those who took part in the death of my great-grandfather, make them pay, let this potion infuse Jacob with a will to kill, a will to contaminate the Montague water source, send the townsfolk into a murderous fury that will rip a gaping wound into the morality of this town, teach it a lesson once and for all that Satanism is not something that will go away, not something to mess with. And only when I say the words—or if my life should one day end—then and only then will this magic spell come to an end. But not before the town is dead."

Her trance-like eyes suddenly refocused and she approached Jacob with the vial.

"No, Jacob," Kathleen said. "Don't drink it. She's going to kill us anyway. I'll die to save the town. Don't, please don't."

Jacob looked at her resolutely. The fear and rage had evaporated from his countenance. "It's okay. I will not stand idly by while my friends die. I made that mistake once."

He opened his mouth, tilted his head and waited. Beatrice emptied the contents into his mouth and he swallowed, spilling a little drop down his chin and onto his naked chest.

It took only a few seconds for his features to change. His eyes became glazed, a dull obedient stare crept across his face. "The mission, master," he said blankly.

"Of course, the mission, my little servant," she said, quickly untying the ropes from his wrists and legs. She pointed to his clothing and he obediently and quickly began dressing.

Kathleen could tell it was no use to say anything. Jacob McCreery was not the same man anymore and she had no idea if he ever would be.

They left. Kathleen could hear the faint voice of Beatrice ushering instructions to her servant, before she heard a vehicle start and then exit the property. She couldn't make out the words but knew well enough what was going to happen. He was on a mission to contaminate the town water supply with Poison Rage. Kathleen had twice witnessed the toxic moonshine's devastating power and she shuddered to think what might happen to an entire town infected by the lethal liquid, and how far the destruction might spread. The death toll would be huge as hundreds of enraged people attacked and killed each other.

They had to stop it. But how?

Mark raised an eyebrow at her suddenly.

"What's up?" she whispered.

"I've got this," he said, opening a palm, exposing the tiny glint of a piece of metal. A razor blade.

Kathleen's countenance brightened. "Where did you get that?"

"I grabbed it in Black Death, before we passed out or were injected or whatever she did to us."

"Can you use it?"

"I've been trying. Look."

She could see the rope binding his right hand just beginning to fray from the back-and-forth motion he was exerting with the razor blade.

Redmond had meanwhile slumped his head to one side again. He appeared to be passed out.

"Redmond, Redmond ... stay with us," Kathleen said.

His eyes slowly opened, his expression dazed. He had lost a lot of blood and barely clung to life.

She gestured with her eyes to Mark and the detective looked beside him. Mark forced a smile, continuing to hack at the rope. "Come hell or high water, we're getting out of here."

A few minutes later, Mark had his right hand free and quickly untied the ropes around his other extremities. He worked with a strength and purpose Kathleen had never before seen, fueled by an adrenaline infusion borne of a need to survive—the fight-or-flight response.

Kathleen pointed to Redmond when Mark freed himself. "Him first."

Even Redmond's eyes were showing signs of a renewed vigor, realizing they had one last kick at the can. It was now or never. Redmond slumped to the ground after he was untied and Mark had to steady him, help him over to the black magic table, where he leaned on it now, inspecting the contents as Mark undid the ropes restricting Kathleen. Redmond shone the flashlight around until he found it—the samurai sword he hadn't gotten the opportunity to use previously.

His face flushing red, he raised the sword above his head and grinned. "That bitch is not getting taken in."

They dressed quickly and Mark was the first to ascend the stairs. He opened the door to bright light of day and was momentarily blinded. He blinked his eyes, adjusting to the light. He heard a click and froze, glancing to his right as Beatrice pulled the trigger on the shotgun and splattered his brain matter onto the door.

He dropped to the ground, what remained of his head spewing blood and twitching spasmodically.

In her haste, Beatrice hadn't been gripping the gun properly, the weapon recoiled and momentarily knocked her off balance. She stumbled back a few steps, trying to regain her balance.

Redmond saw red. He brushed Kathleen aside and raced out the door. Beatrice had by that time regained her balance, reloaded, and was leveling the gun at his head. But Redmond grabbed the barrel just in time, pointing it to the sky and it discharged with a loud blast, burning his hand and sending a round of buckshot airborne.

With a scream, Kathleen knelt over her dead boyfriend, tears streaming down her cheeks. *Let Beatrice kill me now.* At that moment she no longer cared about her life.

Redmond, meanwhile, had tackled Beatrice to the ground. The two rolled in the tall grass on a sunny Monday afternoon, wrestling for control of the shotgun. The samurai sword lay on the grass, glinting in the hot afternoon sun.

"Get the sword," Redmond yelled, the adrenaline dissipating from his body as quickly as it had arrived. He was no match for the unnatural strength of this woman and he was losing the battle for possession of the weapon. Beatrice squatted on top of him and tugged on the shotgun, slowly wresting it from his hands.

No time for mourning, Kathleen suddenly thought. *I want my revenge.*

She picked up the sword, ran swiftly over to the battling pair, raised it and gestured to Redmond. With a sudden elbow to the face from the bottom, he knocked Beatrice off him. She rolled once, the shotgun now firmly in her possession and control. But as she raised it, Kathleen brought the samurai sword down with all her might and cut her aged head clean off.

There was a short, shrill shriek that echoed from her rolling head and then silence and a horror-filled expression as she realized her head had disengaged from her body.

She dropped the shotgun. Her body twitched and went limp.

Redmond stood up dazed, praying for more energy reserves. *Please, one last push.* Someone answered his prayers as he suddenly a felt a renewed strength permeate his body. "Thanks."

"Don't mention it," Kathleen said, staring at what was left of her boyfriend. At least the man she loved had died a hero.

"Check the house," Redmond said. "Look for keys, a phone. I'll see what I can find in the garage. We don't have much time."

Kathleen disappeared into the small and poorly maintained two-story home. Her nostrils were assaulted by a stale odor, the smell of urine mixed with rotting animals, she couldn't be sure. Didn't want to know. She rummaged around a small kitchen table and something jingled under a stack of papers. The keys to Black Death. Where was the truck?

Redmond appeared at the doorway with a red gas can. "I found it. Black Death is covered with a tarp in the garage." Even he was familiar with the truck's nickname by now.

Kathleen appeared at the doorway waving keys and a handgun she had found inside.

"Go get the truck," he said. "I've got unfinished business."

While she ran to the garage, the detective dragged Mark's corpse into the middle of the field. Then he dragged the headless and blood-spewing body of Beatrice up onto the porch. He returned to the lawn, located her head, picked it up by the hair, carried it into the living room and threw it onto a glass coffee table. The coffee table shattered, Beatrice's head landing on the floor underneath a pile of broken glass. Two spears of glass penetrated her eyes, one in each. She looked like a macabre devil.

He stopped to admire his handy work. "You're gonna burn in hell you fucking psychotic witch."

He picked up the gas can and doused Beatrice's head. As he exited he poured a trail of gas to the door. He finished the contents by dumping the remainder onto Beatrice's body. He lit a match and dropped it on the body, just as Kathleen rumbled up in Black Death.

The fire started with a whooshing sound and Redmond had to leap off the porch to avoid getting burned. The flames raced along the gas trail and the house burst into flames.

"Get in," Kathleen said, staring at the corpse of Mark Riley lying in the middle of the field. She was white-knuckled, gripping the wheel and trembling.

"You okay?" Redmond asked as Black Death rolled out of Beatrice's driveway. "You're as white as a sheet."

"No, but thanks for asking. We've got to get to the wells before they're contaminated."

"You know where they are?"

"No."

"I do. You're going the right way. I'll show you where to turn."

"Okay."

They fell silent for a moment, alone with their grief.

"Any phones?" Redmond finally asked as the truck rumbled toward the source of Montague's drinking water.

"No."

"Fuck."

Twenty minutes later they pulled off a highway on the north side of town. "Down that road and to the right where it forks," Redmond said, his voice becoming weaker.

Kathleen floored Black Death and a minute later reached the fork. She veered right so fast the left side wheels became airborne momentarily before they bounced back on the gravel road, skidded for a second, and then found traction and rolled along as she fought to keep the truck on a straight trajectory.

Up in the distance, there was a clearing, surrounded by a chain-link fence topped with coiled barbed wire. There was a lone blue beat-up Chevy pick-up truck parked beside it and the rest of the area was treed. An empty picnic table stood under an overhanging apple tree, a brown steel garbage container beside it.

She skidded to a stop and they exited the vehicle. It didn't take them long to see it. Using wire cutters, Jacob had cut a small opening inside the fence and climbed through the hole. Two small brick buildings were in the middle of a neatly manicured grass field where the wells were located.

Jacob was nowhere to be seen.

Drawing on his last reserves, Redmond checked the chamber of the gun, found it to be loaded and clicked off the safety.

"Jacob," Kathleen said as they approached a brick building with the door hanging open. A padlock had been cut and lay on the grass, alongside a large pair of bolt cutters and a five-gallon clear glass container of yellow liquid. *Maybe we're in time.*

She peered into the brick building and caught Jacob's eyes. He had opened the lid of the well and was positioning a glass container of Poison Rage, when he caught her gaze. "Please leave," he said calmly. "Do not interrupt my mission."

"Freeze," Redmond said. "Don't pour that in there, or I'll shoot."

"It doesn't matter what you do," he said matter-of-factly. "This goes in here."

He tilted the glass jar. Redmond didn't have time to think about it. He fired a bullet into Jacob's chest and he fell back, releasing the jar and slamming into the brick wall where he slumped over, his eyes rolling in his head.

It seemed to her as if everything had happened in slow motion as she reacted. She dove in the air, reaching with both hands for the glass container as it left Jacob's hands and began dropping into the well. And, just when she thought she had her hands wrapped fully around it, everything went black as she felt its wet contents pouring down her hands, suffusing her with an overwhelming and violent urge to kill Detective Blaine Redmond and anyone else she could get her hands on.

Chapter Eighteen

"Here, you put your hands on it like this," Detective Redmond told his wife Jeanette as he lovingly wrapped his hands around hers, explaining the proper way to use a corkscrew.

"Oh." She smiled as he guided her through the motions, and she popped the cork from the bottle of white wine that had been chilling in the refrigerator.

"Should I take it out to our guests or will you?" he asked after kissing her.

"You do it honey. I have to watch the potatoes."

She put on a pair of oven mitts and went over to the oven. She opened the door and peered in.

Six weeks after his traumatic near-death experience, the detective had developed a new appreciation for life. He had vowed to pay more attention to Jeanette if he could only make it out of his ordeal alive. And, since his prayers had been answered, he had made good on his promise. They had become closer than ever, getting along famously and harmoniously, like a couple of newlyweds who had just fallen madly in love.

He had lightened up on the booze, had not been able to give up the cigars, but slowly his life was getting better. No longer preoccupied with death and what he had viewed as failure, he was now content to live every day as if it were his last—try not to preoccupy his mind with the past or the future.

He grabbed a couple of beers from the fridge, walked outside, set the wine bottle and beer on the side of the barbeque, opened the lid and peered in. "It's almost hot enough for the steaks," he told his guests. It was a sunny Sunday afternoon, a day to be appreciated and enjoyed to the fullest.

"I got time for another glass of wine?" Kathleen asked, glancing at Jacob from the corner of her eye. They reclined on bed-style lawn chairs under the shade of a large maple tree.

"Sure do," Redmond said, walking over and handing Jacob a beer and Kathleen the wine bottle.

Jacob popped the can open, took a swig, pulled out a cigar and offered one to the detective. "I have some in the garage," Redmond said.

"No matter," Jacob said. He held out the pack of cigars with his left hand, his right arm still in a sling from the gunshot wound to the shoulder. The bullet had not hit his chest as Redmond had initially thought.

Kathleen filled her wine glass while they lit up. She took a sip and slowly smiled, the comfortable buzz dulling her senses and making everything seem better. And she had to admit, things were a little better than six weeks ago, with the exception of the deaths of Mark and Angela.

Recovering in the hospital from a concussion, she had learned from Redmond that he had pistol-whipped her into unconsciousness after she attacked him with a raging fury.

And he had managed to grab the container and pull it away from the well a split second before the contents spilled into it and contaminated the town's drinking water.

Some of the contents had spilled out on his hands and he had felt himself boiling over with rage. Who knows what would have happened had not Constable Russ Willard, who had since been promoted to detective, shown up and shackled the detective—who had been fit to be tied—into handcuffs and called for back-up.

After being released from the hospital, Jacob and Kathleen had initially been overcome with grief and both decided to take some time off work. They had formed a close and intimate friendship, commiserating and sharing each other's misery and pain. Through it all, Kathleen had weaned herself off the anxiety-attack meds and the metaphor of the calm waters that Betty Shifert had taught her was beginning to help her cope with the feelings of anxiousness.

Of course, she still grieved her loss terribly. And she was still haunted by nightmares of swinging the samurai sword down hard, decapitating Beatrice Maling, watching her blood-spurting head roll across the lawn.

She knew they still had a long way to go. It would probably be a few years before they would be able to get over grieving for their respective spouses. Maybe they'd never get over the loss. Some things just stayed with you for the rest of your life.

And the spirit of Elizabeth Pelletier, the tormented ghost who had removed the perverted spirit of Raymond Dodson, had completely vanished. As if the deed had sapped the last ounce of her spirit energy and she could no longer return to possess Kathleen. As much as she didn't want to admit it, she actually missed the spirit of Liz. At least she knew when Liz was around any paranormal trouble that might emerge would be effectively dealt with.

But the last six weeks had been a quiet period of recovery for Kathleen. There were two requests for paranormal investigations to which she had respectfully declined. After her loss, she didn't think she would ever have the stomach for it again.

Thank God—if there was one—she had her friend Jacob to talk to. Suffering through the same maelstrom of painful emotions, he had been there for her when she needed consoling and vice-versa. Thinking about it now, she wasn't sure she would have gotten through the pain if he hadn't been there to listen and comfort her when she cried. Jacob had even taken her advice and started grief counseling sessions with counselor Betty Shifert, although he jokingly referred to her as "Betty Shit-fer-brains."

He smiled at her suddenly and raised his beer can. "Cheers. To some of the best friends I've ever had."

"Cheers," Kathleen and Redmond said simultaneously, raising their drinks.

"Better include you," Jacob said to Redmond with a wink, "unless I want to get shot."

The detective chuckled and tilted back his beer.

Jeanette appeared at the back door. "Five more minutes and the potatoes will be done. I think you should start the steaks, honey."

"Okay," Redmond said, getting up. Looking at his guests. "That's two medium-rare?"

"Right," Kathleen said.

Jacob nodded, regarding her curiously.

"Why are you looking at me like that?"

"Nothing really. Probably my mind playing tricks on me. I just thought you looked like Angela for a second there."

Dumbfounded, Kathleen stared at Jacob.

"I'm in you and you're in me."

Liz?

"No ... it's me, Angela."

"Oh," Kathleen said. "I didn't realize I look like her."

Also by William Blackwell

Phantom Rage, Poison Rage, Infected Rage
Nightmare's Edge
Resurrection Point
Brainstorm
A Head for an Eye
Rule 14
Blood Curse
Black Dawn
Assaulted Souls
Assaulted Souls II
Assaulted Souls III
The Strap
The End is Nigh
Orgon Conclusion
Freaky Franky
The Witch's Tombstone
The Dark Menace
In Your Dreams
Macabre Alley
Tales of Damnation

Infected Rage, The Rage Trilogy: Book # 3

"The cast of characters, Kathleen, Jacob and Redmond, really leap right off the pages. I like how Blackwell combines psychic and paranormal elements with the zombie-apocalypse story line. Interesting plot and sub-plots along the way, with plenty of shocking twists and turns. The setting, a cold and stormy island, adds to the chilling drama unfolding. Highly recommended reading by a gifted author. You will not be disappointed!!" -Amazon

"It is entertaining and yet creepy in a very unique way. *Infected Rage* surprises the reader over and over again and will shock you to the core." -Goodreads

"I loved everything about this series, from the world, to the characters, to the conflicts, and I highly recommend it to all fans of horror, paranormal novels." -For the Novel Lovers blog

Haunted by the murderous demons of her past, Kathleen Freeborne rips down her shingle as a paranormal investigator and hammers up a new one as a clairvoyant, hoping to better the lives of her shell-shocked clients. Her dreams of a harmonious life are quickly shattered when she feels a man's terrifying rage coursing through her body.

With the help of local police, she investigates disturbing events and learns the shocking truth—a feral animal is infecting locals with a rage virus. Struggling with acute trauma, Kathleen discovers the spread of the virus might be linked to a successful businessman and maybe even government officials. Assembling pieces of a macabre jigsaw puzzle, she learns she is being hunted by a professional hit man.

Adding another layer of terror, her peaceful home is attacked by a pack of frothing, rage-infected zombies. She's plunged into a grueling journey for self-preservation and a search for the horrifying truth behind the rage virus.

About the Author

Canadian dark fiction author William Blackwell studied journalism at Mount Royal University and English literature at The University of British Columbia. He worked as a journalist and a newspaper editor for many years before pursuing his passion for storytelling. His novels have been characterized as graphic, edgy, and at times terrifying. Currently living on a secluded acreage on Prince Edward Island, Blackwell finds much of his inspiration from Mother Nature, odd people, traveling, and bizarre nightmares.

Author Comments

Thank you for reading this book. I would be eternally grateful if you would post a book review on your favorite book retailer website. A positive review is the highest compliment a writer can receive. Reviews are crucial to the success of any author and they help readers discover new books. You don't have to say much. A few sentences will suffice.

In other news, I have a gift for you. Complete the signup form below with your name and email address and download a FREE copy of *Resurrection Point*, a dark tale about the horrifying consequences of experimenting with death and resurrection. You're only agreeing to be kept up to date on blog posts, new releases, and freebies. I promise I won't spam you and you can unsubscribe at any time.

Thanks again for your support.

http://www.wblackwell.com/free-ebook/

www.ingramcontent.com/pod-product-compliance
Lightning Source LLC
Chambersburg PA
CBHW031129210626
46816CB00015B/1259